PUFFIN

STARLIGHT
Stables

BARMAH BRUMBIES

SORAYA NICHOLAS

STARLIGHT
Stables

BARMAH BRUMBIES

PUFFIN BOOKS

PUFFIN BOOKS

UK | USA | Canada | Ireland | Australia
India | New Zealand | South Africa | China

Penguin Books is part of the Penguin Random House group of companies
whose addresses can be found at global.penguinrandomhouse.com.

Penguin
Random House
Australia

First published by Penguin Random House Australia Pty Ltd, 2018

10 9 8 7 6 5 4 3 2 1

Design by Marina Messiha © Penguin Random House Australia Pty Ltd
Cover photograph © Caitlin Maloney, Ragamuffin Pet Photography
Printed and bound in Australia by Griffin Press, an accredited ISO AS/NZS 14001
Environmental Management Systems printer.

A catalogue record for this
book is available from the
National Library of Australia

ISBN 978 0 1437 8743 3 (paperback)

penguin.com.au

For all my wonderful young readers,
who provide such brilliant inspiration for my writing.

CHAPTER ONE

Back in the Saddle

'Go, Poppy, go!'

Poppy's heart pounded in her chest as Crystal's hooves thundered over the grass towards the next jump.

'Go, Pops!'

Poppy stared at the big log ahead of them, steadying Crystal, sitting deeper in the saddle as she pulled back slightly on the reins.

'Come on, girl, we can do it,' she murmured as Crystal's hooves lifted, knees tucking up tight as they cleared the log and landed safely on the other side. The final jump was the ditch, the one she'd been dreading, but she kept her eyes up and her hands steady as they galloped towards it.

She had no idea how many minutes the cross-country course had taken them, but it felt like they'd been flying and Poppy doubted they'd gone over time.

'Good girl,' she whispered. 'Let's do this, we can do this.'

Poppy realised she was pulling back on the reins as Crystal slowed and tossed her head to fight Poppy's control.

Trust her, Poppy. Ride your pony confidently and don't give her your fears.

Aunt Sophie's words rang in her ears and Poppy let the reins slip through her fingers a little, pressing her legs firmly to the pony's sides. Crystal sprang into action, her legs working fast, ears pricked as they rocketed forward. They were only a few strides out and Poppy sat up straight, kept her gaze between Crystal's ears as they lurched upwards and . . . *thud*. They were on the other side!

She slapped Crystal's neck in a big pat, grinning as she leaned forward and pushed her into a full gallop as they raced toward the finishing line.

Within seconds they were through, skidding as

they pulled up to a trot and then a walk. Poppy bent down and threw her arms around Crystal's neck, hugging her as they walked, reins forgotten, her horse's sides heaving against her legs. Crystal's hair was damp against Poppy's cheek, but she didn't care how wet and sweaty her pony was, because they'd made it around perfectly, and she couldn't be more proud of Crystal.

'Way to go, Pops!' Milly was first by her side, high-fiving Poppy as she slowly pushed up off Crystal's neck. Katie joined them, grinning ear to ear, followed by Aunt Sophie. Her aunt beamed proudly as she passed Poppy a bottle of water.

'Crystal was amazing,' Poppy said breathlessly. She guzzled the water gratefully as she took her feet out of the stirrups and stretched out her ankles. Then she passed it back to Sophie and swung down from the saddle, taking Crystal's reins over her head and walking beside her as she headed back to the horse truck.

'Want me to walk her for you?' Katie asked.

'I'd love that,' Poppy said. She felt exhausted, her legs ready to buckle beneath her. She had been one of the last competitors to go around. Milly and

Katie had already ridden the course. Their horses, Joe and Cody, were tied up and munching on hay while they waited for the showjumping phase to start.

'You did great out there, Poppy. I'm so proud of you all today,' Aunt Sophie said, falling into step beside them. 'You're all riding brilliantly, and those ponies of yours couldn't have tried harder for you.'

Poppy grinned at her aunt. Sometimes she could hardly believe it. Less than a year ago, she'd never, *ever* thought she'd own her own horse. Then Aunt Sophie and Uncle Mark had surprised her with beautiful Crystal. Not only that, they'd asked two other young riders – Milly and Katie – to join the Starlight Stables team, and given them horses of their own to ride and train, too. Ever since then, Poppy had been joined at the hip with her new friends – they rode together every other weekend and during the school holidays.

'So, who's going to walk the showjumping course with me?' Aunt Sophie asked. 'I have my pockets lined with Freddo Frogs, so first to . . .'

'Me!' Milly begged, leaping in front of Aunt Sophie and walking backward. 'Anything you want,

I'll do it. Just let me have all the chocolate!'

Poppy rolled her eyes and Katie burst out laughing.

'Oh, Milly, that's so kind,' Aunt Sophie said, winking at Poppy. 'I was going to ask who'd like to be first to muck out around the truck and inside it, and refill the horses' water. Thanks for offering.'

Milly groaned and Poppy exchanged grins with her aunt. Milly drove them crazy sometimes, but she always made them smile.

'Seriously, Mrs D,' Katie said, 'are we all going to walk the course together?'

'Yes,' replied Aunt Sophie. 'We'll check the horses, then head down and go over the course.' She paused. 'I was going to ask who'd like to walk it with me first, but maybe we'll all do it rather than separately.'

'Hang on, so I *don't* have to do all the chores?' asked Milly, hopefully.

Aunt Sophie slung an arm around Milly's neck. 'Of course you don't, silly. That was just payback for trying to cheat your friends out of all the treats.'

Poppy shook her head and smirked at Katie. But Katie was looking at the showjumping course, chewing on her lower lip.

'You nervous?' Katie asked, her voice low.

'It'll be fine. Cody always does well,' said Poppy, putting a hand on her shoulder to try and reassure her.

Katie nodded. 'Yeah, I know. I just really want to go clear.'

'At least your horse didn't put on his brakes and almost send you flying straight over his head on the cross-country course!' said Milly. 'Joe acted like there were monsters hiding in that big brush fence before he changed his mind and lurched over it!'

Katie giggled. Poppy smiled. Trust Milly to make Katie forget all about her worries.

'Girls, do you remember asking me about the Barmah National Park muster a while back?' Aunt Sophie asked suddenly.

The girls all stopped and stared at her. Even Crystal leaned in closer, her nostrils flared, like she was waiting to hear what Sophie was going to say. A shiver of excitement tingled through Poppy. Of course she remembered! When she'd saved her brumby, Storm, they'd researched where he'd come from, and Poppy had begged her aunt and uncle to take them to Barmah one day.

Aunt Sophie obviously took their stunned silence as a yes, because she continued on. 'Unfortunately, we're not going to be able to make the muster.'

Poppy stifled a groan, disappointment pulsing through her. Why had Aunt Sophie even brought it up if it wasn't going to happen?

'Was it my parents?' Katie asked. 'Did they say no to going when you checked with them?'

Aunt Sophie shook her head. 'No, sweetheart, your parents were very excited for you. In fact, all of your parents were happy for you to go.'

Poppy noticed the look on her aunt's face, recognised the slight upturn at the corner of her mouth. She was hiding something from them!

'We can't go on the muster, but we *can* go on the Barmah Heritage Ride.'

They were all silent for a moment as the words sank in.

'What is it? Do we still get to take our own horses there?' Poppy asked.

'*When* is it?' Milly asked.

'Are we *all* going?' Katie cried.

'One at a time, girls!' Aunt Sophie laughed,

holding up her hand. 'Mark and I spoke to a friend at the Victorian Brumby Association, and the heritage ride takes place a week after the muster, so the dates coincide with a long weekend. It's fun and rider focused, which means you get to ride out daily with a mix of experienced and young riders. Mark and I will be coming with you – it's a rule that young riders must be accompanied, so you're stuck with us, but we'll spend five days riding through the forest and camping at the muster yards. It'll be absolutely magical.'

Poppy clamped a hand over her mouth to stop herself from screaming. *Almost a week?* That was awesome news! They were actually going to Barmah!

'So, what do you say?' Aunt Sophie asked. 'If you want to go, it's in three weeks' time, so I should register tonight.'

Poppy threw her arms around her aunt and Milly and Katie did the same, jumping up and down in excitement. 'Thank you!' Poppy squealed. 'Thank you, thank you, thank you!'

'You're the best, Mrs D,' Milly yelled out.

Katie just smiled, her grin stretching ear to ear.

'No need to thank me, girls. But Poppy . . . '

Poppy stopped jumping, wondering what was wrong.

'You might want to go catch your pony.'

Poppy turned and saw Crystal with her head held high, trotting off toward the horse trucks. 'Katie!' she moaned, sprinting after her.

'Sorry!' Katie called out. 'Kind of distracted over here!'

Crystal sped up, racing toward the trucks. There were horse trucks and trailers everywhere, not to mention fancy-looking horses and riders – why did Crystal have to go off on her own at the biggest event she'd ever been to! Poppy groaned. If she stepped on her reins and broke them, she'd kill Katie! Then a slow smile spread across her face. At least she was going in the right direction. And they were going on a *five-day* trail ride through the same park that her brumby, Storm, had originally come from. It didn't get any cooler than that.

Poppy watched from the sidelines as Katie flew around the showjumping course. After walking it together three times over, she was confident she knew the order of the jumps and how many strides were needed between the tricky fences, but actually getting around the course on horseback was something else entirely.

The one-day event was the last of the season, and they had all wanted to do their absolute best. Aunt Sophie had given them horses of their own so they could help promote her riding academy, and Poppy knew she wasn't the only one eager to add more ribbons to the wall in the Starlight Stables tack room.

And if they did well today, Aunt Sophie would decide whether they were ready to move up to the next grade and compete against older riders and jump bigger fences. They would be eligible for junior pre-novice horse trials when the next season started, if they were good enough. A shiver ran down Poppy's spine and she smiled to herself – she loved the challenge and she couldn't wait to jump bigger jumps and keep proving herself to her aunt.

'Go, Katie,' Poppy murmured to herself. 'Only three more to go.'

Katie made it look easy. Cody elegantly soared

over the last few jumps, his canter even and balanced, his head tucked down. They were an amazing team, and even though they were never the fastest, they usually always went around clear without touching a pole.

Milly had already ridden, flying around the course at a mad pace and no doubt beating all of them in the speed stakes. But she'd taken two rails, which she had been disappointed about.

Poppy gritted her teeth and collected her reins, nudging Crystal forward with her heels and heading for the training area now that she'd seen Katie finish. She pushed her pony into a trot and they did a few circles, but when Crystal started tossing her head and trying to run off, Poppy switched gears and made her slow down, riding some figure of eights and then serpentines to get her to settle. Aunt Sophie had always told Poppy that Crystal was excitable and got bored quickly, which meant she had to get her thinking to make her calm down.

Once they'd found a nice rhythm, Poppy sat deep and asked Crystal to canter. Being one of the last competitors to go was nice, because there weren't many riders competing for the warm-up area, and it gave her time to settle Crystal and practise going over a few jumps without having to watch out for other horses.

Crystal rushed over the first practice fence but Poppy forced her to slow again, sitting deep in the saddle and keeping her hands firm. They cantered around for a second time, careful to give another horse a wide berth as they circled and approached again.

'Good girl!' Poppy praised her this time, patting Crystal's neck and then turning her in a circle and heading back in the other direction. They shot forward and cantered toward the jump, clearing it again.

Poppy slowed Crystal to a trot and let the reins slide through her fingers, allowing her to stretch her neck out. They trotted for a while longer before walking and then finally making their way back toward the showjumping ring.

'Competitor sixty-nine? Do we have competitor sixty-nine? Poppy Brown?' an official called out, tapping her pen against her clipboard.

'Here!' Poppy called, riding closer.

'You're up,' the woman instructed. 'We've had

a few riders scratched from the program, so you're on next.'

A tremor of excitement ran through Poppy and she placed a hand on Crystal's neck. They'd trained hard for this event, there was no reason for her to be so nervous, but still her stomach always started to flip whenever they were about to compete.

The rider who'd been in the ring exited and Poppy gathered up her reins and urged Crystal on, pushing her pony straight into a trot and then a bouncy canter. They circled, waiting for the bell to jingle, and when it did she took a deep breath, circled one more time, then headed for the first jump.

Poppy's stomach was still churning as they approached, but the moment they flew over the simple upright her nerves miraculously disappeared and her head went silent. She couldn't hear anything other than the rise and fall of her own breath, and Crystal's hoof beats and then low grunt as they cleared another jump. It was always like that for her – once she was in the ring she never thought about anything other than riding clear. And winning.

The next one was wider, an oxer, and Crystal

sped up, taking off earlier than expected but still clearing it easily. Poppy pushed her heels down hard and lifted out of the saddle, feeling clumsy as they landed and almost losing her stirrup. But she didn't have time to worry. There was another vertical ahead and then the combination.

'We're doing great,' she whispered to Crystal. 'Whoa, girl. Whoa now.'

She didn't want to go too fast into the two jumps ahead. There were only two strides between each one and she didn't want to muck up the first and end up crashing through the second. They were steady, Crystal was pulling hard against her hands, but within seconds they were airborne and Poppy released the reins, giving Crystal her head as they cleared it.

One, two . . . Yes! They were over the second jump. They had a wall ahead to jump, then another oxer.

'Let's do this!' she told Crystal as they rocketed forward.

Poppy was confident now, loving the feel of her powerful pony beneath her, and Crystal's ears were pricked, enjoying the show jumping as much as the rider. Poppy knew it was like a game to Crystal, one she liked to play fast.

They jumped all the final fences, flying over the last one with ease. The small crowd clapped and Poppy beamed, her cheeks aching from smiling so hard. They'd done it!

'Yes! Good girl!' she praised, fighting to slow Crystal down and exiting the ring at a way-too-fast trot. She bumped in the saddle trying to get her to walk, but it wasn't until they were back near the warm-up area that Crystal finally calmed down. Her nostrils were flared and her steps still fast, but the jig-jogging had stopped.

Poppy took her boots from the stirrups and stretched her ankles out, walking for a while before halting and dismounting. She stroked Crystal's face, dropping a kiss to her cheek, before running up her stirrups and loosening the girth a little.

'We did great today,' she told Crystal as they walked.

She opened her mouth to say something else but saw Milly running towards them, flapping her hands, and Katie just behind her. She grinned and waved at her friends. When she finally reached them, Milly looked like she was about to burst.

'We need to do a practice camp out,' Milly announced, eyes wide as she grabbed Poppy's hand. 'We can ride out with a tent and . . .'

'Um, I think you should have started that with telling Poppy how crazy-amazing she was out there,' Katie scolded.

Poppy bit down on her lip and stroked Crystal's neck. 'You really think so?'

Katie grinned. 'I know so. You were fast *and* clear.'

Milly laughed. 'Yeah, yeah, we know Poppy's amazing. You *were* awesome out there,' she said quickly. 'But what about the camping? How cool would it be to ride through the farm and have a night out? Just us! We can tell Mrs D that we need a practice run.'

Poppy did have to admit that it sounded kind of fun. 'So without Sophie and Mark?'

'Just us,' Milly said. 'Well, our horses too obviously, but it'd be so much fun.'

'And you want me to ask if we can do it?' Poppy said, knowing that's why Milly was asking her.

'Yup,' Milly replied.

Katie's smile was wide; she was clearly as excited about the whole thing as Milly. 'Guys, if we stand around talking any longer, we're going to miss finding out who's going home with a ribbon!'

Poppy gulped. A little voice in her head was whispering that she might get a ribbon, but she pushed the thought away, not wanting to get her hopes up, and smiled back at her friends. 'What are we waiting for?' she blurted. 'Let's go!'

They hurried off toward the showjumping ring. Volunteers had already begun to disassemble the jump stands and candy-striped poles, and as the girls stopped behind the rest of the crowd a loudspeaker crackled.

Chills tingled through Poppy and she was relieved when Aunt Sophie appeared in the crowd and made her way back to them.

'We'll start by announcing sixth place, which goes to . . . Amelia Walker!'

Poppy slapped Milly on the back as she leapt forward, beaming, to go and collect her ribbon. The announcer announced fifth place, and then fourth, and Katie grabbed Poppy's hand, her fingers digging in tight. Surely they were going to place?

Did she actually have a chance of winning?

'In third place we have Katie Richards!'

Katie let out a little squeal of delight as she rushed forward. It was just Aunt Sophie and Crystal standing with her now, and Sophie's hand brushed her shoulder before she took the reins from her.

'I'm so proud of you, Pops,' Aunt Sophie whispered. 'You and Crystal are showing the signs of being amazing competitors.'

'Thank you,' she whispered back, ready to burst from the praise and the excitement of it all.

Poppy held her breath, unable to push it out. Would she get second place? They'd ridden so well, and if Katie had made third place then . . .

'Second place goes to Lily McBreen!'

She didn't get it. Her heart sunk. Maybe her morning dressage hadn't been good enough? Maybe it was stupid to think she'd done so well? She wrapped her arms tightly around herself.

'And, finally, first place goes to Poppy Brown riding Starlight Crystal!'

Poppy froze. *First place?* She'd actually won first place?!

'Poppy, go!' Aunt Sophie urged.

Poppy stumbled forward. She'd done it. She'd made Aunt Sophie proud. Starlight Stables had taken out three of the six ribbons, and moving up a grade would take her one step closer to her dream of being in the Australian junior rider squad when she was older. She couldn't stop grinning.

CHAPTER TWO

Starlight Fun

Poppy sat on the grass with Crystal's head cradled in her lap. She'd been sitting there for ages, but she didn't dare move. Her pony made a soft snorting noise and she stroked her face, smoothing down her forelock and then running her fingertips across her cheek. She wished Aunt Sophie could see this special moment, could see how trusting Crystal was with her as she slept.

'We're going on an adventure soon,' she whispered to Crystal, trying to wiggle her toes. Her legs were starting to feel numb from having her horse's heavy head on her for so long, but she didn't care. It had been two weeks since they'd won the event, and she'd missed being with Crystal – she'd had to stay in town for a school fundraiser the weekend before. 'We're going to camp out and go on trail rides and look for wild horses! Only seven more sleeps to go!'

Her excited mutterings made Crystal's ears prick, and when the pony lifted her head and looked at her, Poppy smiled. She knew that Crystal couldn't understand her words, but sometimes Poppy wondered if her pony knew more than she realised.

'Hello, sleepyhead,' Poppy said, scooting back on her bottom as Crystal stretched out her front legs. She stood, waiting until Crystal finished stretching, and then she climbed onto her back. As Crystal stood, Poppy carefully balanced, laughing at the funny sensation of Crystal rising. Then she did a big full body shake and Poppy grasped her mane tight as she shook from side to side. 'Guess that serves me right for making you stand up with me on your back,' she muttered, touching her legs to Crystal's sides and guiding her forward. They had an amazing bond now, and being able to ride her bareback and tell her where to go with just her legs felt incredible.

'Don't go worrying about me choosing Storm over you, either,' she continued to chat to Crystal, one hand resting on her wither, the other on her own thigh. 'I think Aunt Sophie will ride him when we go to Barmah. I want to have fun with you.'

Poppy hated being torn between the two horses, because she loved them both. But Crystal was her riding horse, the pony of her dreams, and they were a team. Storm was amazing, but he was still too much of a handful for Poppy to ride on her own, and she didn't have the same super-close bond with him yet. Plus Aunt Sophie would be able to deal with any naughty antics, especially if he freaked out at being back in his home forest.

'Poppy, where's your helmet?' Aunt Sophie called out.

Poppy quietly said 'whoa' to Crystal and slipped to the ground. She braved a smile and met Sophie's gaze. How had she not seen her aunt standing there, leaning on the gate, with Crystal's halter and rope slung over her shoulder?

'Sorry. I didn't actually plan on riding her,' Poppy mumbled.

'I saw you wriggle up on her when I came along,'

Sophie said, her brows raised. 'I'll spare you a telling off this time, but only because I'm so proud of the way you two have clicked as a team lately. And while I'm on that topic, your riding at the last event was amazing. I can't see any reason why you and Crystal can't move up to pre-novice next season, Pops.'

Poppy stared at her, stunned. She was moving up!

'Thanks, Aunt Sophie,' she stammered finally. Then she started to laugh, clamping a hand over her mouth to try and stop herself. 'Sorry, but I just can't believe it. I'm so excited!'

'So you should be! You've done great and you deserve it.'

Sophie was holding Crystal's halter and Poppy took it from her and put it on Crystal, working the buckles quickly and then picking up the end of the lead rope that had already been clipped on.

'So, tell me, am I still allowed to take your Storm on this trail ride?' Aunt Sophie asked, holding the gate open for her so she could lead Crystal through.

'Of course!' Poppy replied. 'I'd love him to go back to the place he came from.'

'Good, because I'm looking forward to doing some more work with him,' Aunt Sophie said. 'And it'll be good for him to be ridden out in a group like that. He's been coming along nicely these last few weeks.'

Poppy hadn't seen Sophie working Storm yet under saddle, but she was looking forward to watching how well he was doing.

'Aunt Sophie, I know he's really young and inexperienced, but . . .' Poppy gulped, finding it hard to say the words.

'Spit it out, Pops.'

'I just, well, I'd love to ride him when you think he's ready and I'm ready and . . .'

'That's what you were spluttering about? Wanting to ask if you could ride your own horse?'

Poppy shrugged, feeling silly. 'Yes.' Secretly she was worried he'd start thinking Aunt Sophie was his rider. Even though she spent heaps of time with him, her aunt had been the one training him and riding him while she was at school. She wanted to make sure they had a special bond, just like she did with Crystal.

Aunt Sophie laughed as they walked together toward the stables, Crystal between them. 'I'd love you to ride him. How about we go catch him and have a quick lesson before your friends arrive? There's no better day to start than today.'

Poppy beamed back at her aunt, holding in a squeal of excitement. Just when she'd thought her morning couldn't get any better . . .

Poppy ran the brush over Storm's dark, almost black coat. He quivered when she pushed past the groove at his flank and she placed her other hand on his back to steady him.

'It's okay,' she said in a low voice. 'You're just fine.'

He bent around and nuzzled her bottom and she laughed as his top lip hardened. She knew exactly what he wanted. Poppy scratched him on his back, moving her fingers until she found the spot he liked. She giggled as he frantically tried to scratch her back, his top lip moving back and forth against her jodhpurs.

'Thanks,' she muttered, trying to move away from him but not succeeding. He was desperate to scratch her in return and he wasn't taking no for an answer!

'What's going on in there?'

Aunt Sophie's head popped over the stall door and Poppy stopped scratching Storm.

'He thinks I'm a horse and he wants to scratch with me,' she said. 'It's so crazy that I can trust him like this now. A month ago I'd have thought he was going to take a bite out of my butt!'

Sophie smiled and stepped into the stall to brush Storm's face. 'He's turned out to be a really lovely horse, Pops,' she said. 'You had good instincts when you bought him.'

Poppy shook her head, embarrassed. 'No, I didn't. I just felt really sorry for him when I saw him in those awful auction yards.'

But she *had* seen something else, a spark of something special, a determination in his eyes that told her he deserved to live.

Sophie touched her arm. 'He's a good horse, Poppy. There's a reason you fell in love with him, I think.'

Poppy finished brushing his body and took the saddle down from the door where it had been resting.

'Go more slowly with him than you do with

Crystal,' Aunt Sophie said. 'He's doing well, but he's still very green, and that means we need to make our movements slow and steady, especially when we're doing his girth or asking him to open his mouth for the bit.'

Poppy did as she was told, easing the saddle on and being careful to check it was sitting properly before tightening the girth. She made it firm enough to hold the saddle, but it would need to go up a notch or two before she rode him.

Her aunt stood back as she coaxed the bit into his mouth with ease and did up the throat lash and then the noseband.

'Good boy,' Poppy murmured softly. She turned to look at Aunt Sophie. 'What next?'

'Now I'll lead him out while you put your helmet on,' she said. 'And then you're up.'

Goose pimples prickled across Poppy's arms. She'd sat on him bareback, and walked around, but to actually ride him properly? She shivered. It was scary but exciting at the same time.

She reached for her helmet where she'd left it outside the stable and put it on, checking it was firm. The last thing she wanted to do was muck anything up when it came to Storm – she wanted him to love her as much as she already loved him.

'Up you get,' Aunt Sophie said, placing Storm's reins over his head and keeping hold of him.

Poppy took a deep breath and gave him a pat before checking his girth.

'Just mount like normal. It's good to land nice and softly in the saddle.'

Poppy placed her foot in the stirrup iron and pushed up, landing with a gentle thud and taking up her reins. Her heart was banging away in her chest, but she braved a smile at Aunt Sophie.

'Ready?' Sophie asked.

'Yup. Ready,' Poppy replied. 'Do I just ask him to walk out like I do with Crystal?'

'Absolutely. Just don't ask too much, and keep a firm but gentle contact with his mouth.' Aunt Sophie placed a hand on her leg. 'And I'm here with you every step of the way, so you don't have to be nervous.'

Poppy nodded and looked ahead as they walked out into the sun. Storm tossed his head and fidgeted nervously. He felt different beneath her, his strides slightly longer than Crystal's, his head held high as he stepped out. Both horses were a similar size, so it was weird how different they felt.

'You're doing great,' Aunt Sophie said as they neared the arena. 'I'm going to stand in the middle, just like I usually do during a lesson. You can walk him around a bit, then when you feel ready, ask him to trot.'

Poppy smiled to herself as they walked around. She could hardly believe she was up on Storm! Only two months ago he'd been almost completely wild and terrified of humans. Now, he was behaving like any other well-trained young horse.

After walking for a while, she nudged her legs to his sides and clucked him on. 'Trot on,' she asked.

He burst into a fast, bouncy trot, and Poppy focused on rising and falling in the saddle, doing her best to settle him. She glanced over at her aunt and received a smile in return, so she figured she was doing okay.

When Poppy decided to change the rein, going in the opposite direction to what she was going in, she crossed through the centre of the arena. As they were turning back onto the track she pressed her legs to his sides, wanting to keep the momentum going, but Storm confused her nudge and cantered.

'Just trotting,' Poppy murmured to him, trying to pull him back gently into a trot, but Storm had other ideas. He let loose a buck, his back legs kicking up and out in a motion so fast it almost unseated Poppy. 'Hey!' she scolded. 'That's enough!'

Storm slowed and trotted again, but he was tossing his head now and Poppy was finding him harder to control. When she demanded that he walk and then halt, he pawed at the ground and started to walk backwards, making a fuss. She had no idea what to do.

'Um, Sophie?' she asked, trying to keep the waver out of her voice.

'You're fine. Just make him walk on. Don't stop. Keep him moving forward.'

'But I want to stop!' Poppy pleaded, panic rising in her chest. She felt like she was going to suffocate. Why wouldn't he stop? Why was he being so silly?

'Ask him to walk on, get him thinking. You can't let him behave like that,' Aunt Sophie said. 'If you get off now, he'll think he's won and that he's the one in charge. This isn't like him, but he's testing you. All young horses do it every now and again.'

Poppy listened to her aunt and knew that what she said was true. She squared her shoulders. She could do this. Storm was her horse and she was the boss. She breathed deep, refusing to let him rattle her.

'Walk on,' she demanded, her voice firm as she coaxed him forward. 'Good boy.' She quickly praised him when he did what was asked.

Storm snorted but he walked forward, and when she asked him to trot, he did that, too. Poppy rode him around, doing figure of eights and changing direction through the centre of the arena before finally asking him to walk again. This time, he listened, even when she gave the command to halt.

As soon as he was perfectly still, she patted his neck and briskly dismounted. She'd done what Aunt Sophie had asked her to do, acting way more brave than she'd actually felt, but now she was ready to get off. And fast.

'Well done,' Aunt Sophie said. 'He was testing you and you showed him exactly who was in charge.'

'I didn't know what to do,' Poppy admitted. 'I . . .' Her voice went wobbly and she couldn't stop it.

Aunt Sophie took the reins from her shaking hands. 'That's why you're riding him with me nearby. It's only a disaster if you're on your own and don't know how to react. Pops, you did great, and because you handled it so well it's unlikely he'll bother trying those kind of tricks on you again. It was just bad luck he tried it on your first proper ride together!'

Poppy smiled. She was just relieved it was over! Crystal could be a handful sometimes and often felt explosive beneath her, but in a safe way. She was just excitable. Storm was a young horse playing up, whereas Crystal would never try to throw her off or hurt her intentionally. Poppy was relieved her aunt would be riding him at Barmah, because if he freaked out there, she wouldn't have a clue what to do!

'Give him some time,' Aunt Sophie said, as if she'd known exactly what Poppy was thinking. 'Before you know it he'll be just like Crystal and all the other horses you've ridden. Young horses take a lot of training and a lot of patience. Especially wild ones.' She laughed.

'Now go and join your friends. Milly looks like

she's about to die of boredom waiting over there!'

Poppy looked over her shoulder and saw her friends watching from the other side of the arena. She'd been so focused on Storm that she hadn't even noticed them. She held up her hand in a wave. 'Want me to take Storm back first?' Poppy asked, turning back to Aunt Sophie.

She shook her head. 'I'm going to do a little more work with him. Go see your friends and be saddled up in an hour for your group lesson.'

Poppy stepped back and gave Storm a quick pat before running over to Milly and Katie.

'Hey,' she said, slinging an arm around each of them.

'Were you scared riding him?' Katie asked as they walked down to where Cody and Joe were grazing. They automatically headed straight there whenever they arrived.

'Um, well, maybe just a little.'

'Liar!' Milly teased. 'You were absolutely terrified up there. I saw your face.'

Poppy giggled. 'Okay, so I was scared. He felt really tight beneath me and all coiled up, and when I couldn't make him stand still, I totally freaked.'

Milly sighed. 'You do realise you were nuts to take on a brumby, right?'

'You do realise we're nuts to be friends with you, but we are anyway, right?' Poppy teased straight back.

'So are we going practice camping tonight?' Milly asked impatiently, lead rope over her shoulder as she swung the end of it. 'I brought all my stuff!'

Poppy felt her smile drop. They'd been texting each other since the event about doing a camp-out tonight, and Katie had messaged them a huge list of what they needed to bring for it, even though they were only going for one night. But in all the excitement of riding Storm she'd totally forgotten to ask Aunt Sophie if they could do it!

'Poppy!' Katie scolded, seeing her face. 'You promised!' She opened the gate and marched off to catch Cody.

'*Please,* Poppy,' Milly begged, hands pressed together in front of her like she was praying. 'It'll be so much fun – we have to go.'

Poppy smiled. 'So long as it's more fun than the time we snuck off to look for those stolen horses.'

'Hey, that time we were *sneaking*. This time, we

won't be getting into any trouble.'

Poppy watched as Milly raced off, leaping over the fence, her curls bouncing as she ran. That was half the problem, she thought. Whenever Milly suggested anything, it *always* ended up being trouble.

But it *would* be awesome to camp out together. The weather was perfect, they could ride out and find a good spot to put up their tents, and the horses would love going for a nice long walk after their lesson. She'd eagerly packed everything in her overnight bag as well.

She watched Milly and Katie haltering their horses for a moment and then sprinted off to ask her aunt if they could do it, pumping her arms as she raced back down to the arena. She arrived just in time to see Storm give a massive buck and almost send Sophie flying over his head.

Poppy winced as her brumby was scolded, happy that she hadn't been on his back when he'd done that! It looked like he had a lot more training to go . . .

CHAPTER THREE

Adventure Planning

'She said yes!' Poppy thudded into the stable door.

'No way!' Milly called out from inside Joe's stable. 'After our lesson?'

'So long as we do our chores before going and stay within, like, a fifteen-minute ride of the house, she said it was fine.' Poppy laughed. 'She even said we could stay out until early afternoon tomorrow if we wanted to. The only catch is that we have to text her and keep a phone on us the whole time. Oh, and she was super impressed we had everything packed to take.'

'Awesome!' Milly's excitement was palpable through the stall doors.

'Can we take Casper?' Katie called out. 'Don't you guys remember that I'm scared of the dark?'

Poppy groaned. 'There's nothing out there to be scared of, silly!'

'Nothing to be scared of?' Katie's head appeared over the stable door. 'Um, have you heard of snakes and wild animals and, oh, you remember Old Man Smithy? We could die out there!' she said dramatically.

It wasn't like Katie to be such a drama queen. That was usually Milly's role.

'We'll be fine,' Poppy said, picking up a brush and starting to groom Crystal. 'If it wasn't safe, Aunt Sophie would never let us go.'

'I still think we should take Casper with us,' Katie said.

Poppy chewed on her lip as she thought, brushing Crystal's leg firmly to get rid of some dirt. 'I don't know. Remember that time we stayed the night in here and he just slept through all the scary noises anyway?'

Milly's laughter boomed across the stables. 'Yeah, he'll be more trouble than he's worth. I vote we leave him behind.'

'This is going to be *so* cool,' Poppy crowed. She finished brushing Crystal, then saddled her and bridled her. What would they take? How long would they be gone? When she finally emerged from the stable at the same time as Milly, she couldn't stop grinning.

'I wish we didn't have a lesson first,' Milly said, groaning as she mounted.

Poppy shrugged. 'It'll be fun. I'm just happy to be back in the saddle again.' Poppy never cared what kind of riding she was doing, so long as she was on horseback.

'Do you guys think we should go over our list?'

'No!' Milly insisted, flicking her whip at Katie. 'This is not something you need to over-organise, okay?'

Poppy tried not to giggle. Milly was so bossy sometimes and poor Katie just liked to have everything planned out. 'I think we'll be fine with just some food, water, a tent and –'

'There's one thing we forgot about!' Katie said. 'We need something to pen the horses in or to tether them with.'

'I'll get some fencing tape,' said Poppy. 'We can

wind it around some trees or something, and it'll be light to carry.'

They rode out into the bright sunlight together.

'Come on, let's trot down,' said Poppy. 'The quicker our lesson's over, the quicker we can get our chores done and get ready to go!'

She made a low clucking sound and touched her heels to Crystal's sides to get her to trot, reins loose so she could stretch out. The others quickly caught up to her and they rode three abreast down to the arena.

'You girls ready to go?'

Poppy turned to see Uncle Mark leaning against the kitchen door, smiling. He had Ghost, the once-wild black cat they'd found in the barn, tucked up in one arm, and the other hand was holding a packet of chips.

'Just about,' Poppy said, looking down at her bulging backpack.

'Well, these are for you,' he said, passing her the chips. 'Do you have enough other food?'

'Um, I think we'll be okay, Mr D,' said Katie

gravely. 'We've made sandwiches for dinner and we have plenty of snacks.'

Poppy smirked. They had enough snacks to last them a week.

Milly held out the tent bag that Katie had brought with her. 'So, one of you guys actually knows how to put this thing up, right?'

Poppy laughed. 'Not me,' she replied.

Katie waved her hand in the air. 'Piece of cake. I've gone camping lots with my brothers, and I'm always the one who helps dad put our tent up. We'll be fine.'

'So can we go now?' Milly asked. 'Actually, can we eat first? I'm starving.'

'You're always starving,' Poppy teased. 'Here, let's eat these. Then we're going.'

She ripped open the bag of chips and grabbed a handful before passing it over to Milly. They munched in silence for a bit, and Poppy licked the chicken flavouring off her fingers as Katie offered some to Uncle Mark.

'Is there anywhere you'd recommend we set up camp?' she asked him. 'Like under a tree or out in the open or near water for the horses?'

Uncle Mark put Ghost down. 'Water is a great idea. Why don't you ride over near the creek? Pops, that's still one of your favourite places, isn't it?'

She nodded, imagining straightaway the lovely little spot where they could set up camp. 'Uh-huh. Sounds good to me.'

'We need to run quickly through all the boring stuff before you go though, girls. Listen up.'

Milly jumped up and down impatiently and Poppy grabbed her arm. 'Stop it,' she growled.

Milly rolled her eyes, but she stayed still.

'Poppy, your phone must stay with you and be turned on at all times, and you girls should take yours just in case as back-up,' Uncle Mark began. 'No riding anywhere else but straight down to the creek, and if anything changes you need to call for permission first. If you're unsure about anything or if you're scared, text or call me and I'll drive down to get you, and if there's an accident, the first thing you do is pick up the phone. Understood?'

'Yes, sir!' they chorused together.

'You have food, water, torches and warm clothes?' he asked.

'Yep, all of that. Can we go now?' Milly asked.

Mark laughed and threw his hands in the air in surrender. 'Go. And have fun!'

The girls rushed to put their packs on and headed for the stables. Milly had the tent in her big pack, Katie had sleeping-bags in her pack, and Poppy had their food and water. They weren't taking a lot, but it was still heavy on her back. She'd try to remember to apologise to Crystal for the extra weight.

'Bye, girls!' Aunt Sophie called out. She was leading her huge Warmblood gelding Jupiter, and his rich chestnut coat gleamed in the sunshine. He lifted his big, noble head, ears pricked, watching them as they ran past.

Poppy waved. 'Bye!'

'See you tomorrow!' Katie called out.

'See ya, Mrs D!' Milly yelled back.

Poppy smiled at her friends, excitement buzzing through her. They were actually going to spend the night out on their own with their horses, with no adults.

She squared her shoulders and tucked her fingers beneath the straps of her pack. Something about being totally in charge of what she did for the next twenty-four hours was making her feel super grown-up, and she liked it.

'Race to the horses?' Milly asked.

Before they could answer, she took off. Poppy raced to catch up with her, but her pack was just too heavy. Milly looked like a turtle, the tent pack swaying from side to side and threating to overbalance her.

Katie's giggles echoed her own as they reached the stables behind Milly and thumped into the wall.

'We need to stop letting her beat us like that,' Katie panted to Poppy.

Milly planted her hands on her hips and grinned at them. 'Never!'

Once they'd caught their breath, Poppy ducked into the storage room to grab the roll of electric fence tape Aunt Sophie had told them to take. Then they went to get their ponies.

Crystal was still saddled up, and Poppy put a brush in her backpack before zipping it up and checking her straps were firm. She did the same to her girth then tied the lead rope from Crystal's halter on to her saddle. They would need their halters later so she'd left it on over the bridle.

'Ready?' she called out to the others before pushing open her stable door.

'Ready!' Milly and Katie called out at the same time, their doors creaking as they led their ponies out to join her.

'Let the fun begin!' Milly announced.

Poppy led Crystal out into the sunlight and mounted. Excitement pulsed through her and she looked expectantly at her friends. It was time to go!

They set off at a walk and Poppy held her reins on the buckle, content to let Crystal stretch out and relax, enjoying the gentle sway of her horse beneath her. She was usually eager to canter and find logs to jump, but today their packs were heavy and she knew the horses were tired. They'd spent an hour with Aunt Sophie concentrating on dressage and jump training, and her own legs ached.

She glanced back, trying to catch a glimpse of Storm in his paddock, but she couldn't see him. A pang echoed through her chest, and she felt guilty that he wasn't with them. Sometimes it was tough loving two horses.

'What do you think the trail ride will be like at Barmah?' Katie asked. 'Do you think we'll actually see a mob of wild brumbies? I can't believe we're going!'

Poppy sighed. 'I really, really hope so. It'd be so magical. Tomorrow when we wake up it'll only be six more sleeps!'

'Do you think they just gallop off when they see people, or do you think it'll be like in the movies and they'll look up and silently watch us?' Katie said with a sigh.

Milly laughed. 'I hope it's like the movies!'

Poppy could imagine exactly what it would be like. There'd be a small mob and they'd all pause from grazing, looking up with their steady, deep gazes. Then Storm would whinny out to them, knowing they were his own kind, that this was the place he'd come from, and then the mob would slowly disappear into the trees.

She'd read so much about Barmah when she'd first bought Storm, and since they'd found out they were going she'd looked up everything she could find all over again. It was going to take them a couple of hours to drive there next Saturday, and she'd read that locals and the government couldn't agree on how many horses were left in the wild there. Some said 100 horses lived there, and others claimed it was 300, so she wasn't sure what to believe. She couldn't wait to ride through the forest and see the river, and try to spot as many different kinds of wild animals as she could.

'Poppy?'

She blinked and looked over at Katie. 'Sorry, what?'

'She was daydreaming,' Milly said. 'We just go straight down here to ride to the creek, right?'

'Yep,' Poppy said, stroking Crystal's neck as they walked. She should have been tired and slow, but instead her pony was striding out fast, excited about going on a bigger ride. 'There's a cluster of trees a little bit further away from the big old Oak near the creek. We could put our tape around that and pen the horses there for the night.'

'Sounds perfect,' Katie replied. 'You know, I'm still a bit scared of staying out tonight, but it was a good idea, Mils. This is kind of fun being out just the three of us.'

'So my ideas aren't always crazy, is that what you're saying?' Milly asked.

'Well . . . '

Poppy smiled as she listened to her friends, closing her eyes for a moment and feeling her horse moving beneath her, the rhythm so natural to her now. Being on horseback was her happy place. When she opened her eyes they were riding through a big cluster of gums. She looked up at the beautiful pale, bleached trunks stretching effortlessly high into the air, leaves waving in the light breeze, forming an umbrella above them. She was looking forward to going away for the week to Barmah, but she doubted that anywhere in the world would be better to ride than her aunt and uncle's farm.

Milly and Katie were still chatting beside her as she stared ahead, smiling to herself when she saw a kangaroo straighten, then another three beside it. They sniffed the air then hopped off, unhurried but putting distance between them. She wondered if that's what it would be like seeing the brumbies in the wild.

It took them almost twenty minutes to ride to the creek at a slow walk, which had just enough water for the horses to splash their hooves and take a shallow drink. Poppy reluctantly dismounted once Crystal had dipped her head and sipped her fill.

She could have stayed in the saddle for hours.

'Who's in charge of what?' Poppy asked, looking at her friends. 'Katie, if you want to put up the tent, maybe Milly could help you and I could do the tape fence for the horses.'

'How about I do the fence?' Milly asked. 'If I have anything to do with the tent, it'll definitely collapse in the middle of the night!'

Poppy grinned. 'Good point. Let's tether them to the branches over there –' she pointed, '– and you can put the temporary fence up around them. We can dump our bags and stuff here.' She took off her pack and set it down, then led Crystal over to the trees.

Milly tied Joe up and began fumbling around with the tape. Poppy left her to it, taking Crystal's saddle and bridle off and propping them on the other side of the tree, then moving around to Joe and doing the same for him. She fell into step beside Katie, who had finished unsaddling Cody, and they started hunting around for a good spot to set up the tent.

'Do you think there'll be possums around tonight?' Katie asked, her eyes wide.

Poppy linked her hand through Katie's arm and shook her head. 'Look, we'll be so tired tonight that we'll fall asleep before we even hear any animals. And no, I don't think there will be any around. They're way more scared of us than we are of them, remember?'

Katie didn't look convinced. 'Let's just get this tent up. The only thing worse than being out here at night in a tent would be *not* having a tent to hide in!'

Poppy stifled a laugh and unzipped the tent bag, hoping for Katie's sake that they didn't have any animal encounters during the night. She had no idea what she was doing when it came to tents – it had been years since she'd been camping and back then her dad had been in charge of things like that. She blinked back tears when the familiar prickle pierced her eyes. Most days she didn't think about him, not when she was busy, but it was little odd things like this that brought back a flood of memories.

'You all right?'

'Yeah. It's just, well, the last time I went camping was with my dad.'

Katie stared at her, like she wasn't sure what

to say, then she suddenly dropped what she was holding and leaped over the tent bag, swallowing Poppy in a huge hug.

'I'm sorry, Pops,' she whispered in her ear, holding her tight.

Poppy hugged her back, feeling better and gulping a big breath before stepping away. 'Now, let's get this tent up.'

Katie stared at her for a second, like she was checking she was actually okay, before nodding and going back to the tent. They laughed and tripped and giggled while they fumbled to erect it, but they finally managed to get it up.

'Not bad,' Milly said from behind them.

Poppy spun, hands on her hips, proud of their handiwork. The tent was a tiny bit lopsided, but other than that it looked perfect. 'Yeah, we did great, Katie!'

They got their sleeping-bags out, and crawled into the tent to lay them out. They just fitted side by side. Poppy bundled up her hoodie as a pillow. It wasn't going to be the most comfortable sleep in the world, but as she traded smiles with the others, she knew it was going to be a heap of fun.

CHAPTER FOUR

Double Disaster

Poppy passed around sandwiches before taking her own out and unwrapping it. Her stomach growled. The horses were happily munching grass, the tent was up behind them, and Poppy was sitting side by side with her friends as the sun slowly disappeared for the day. The air was cooler than it had been earlier, a slight chill sending a ripple of tiny goose pimples across her bare arms.

'This is so cool,' Milly said between mouthfuls. 'I get sick of my parents telling me what to do all the time, and my teacher telling me to listen and stop talking, and . . .'

'You do talk too much,' Poppy laughed. 'I bet

you drive your teacher absolutely nuts.'

Milly glared at her. 'I do *not* talk too much,' she huffed.

'I know what you mean though. It's kind of nice and silent out here, just being us.'

Poppy loved her mum, and she liked school most of the time, but it was kind of awesome being trusted to go out alone for the night with no adults in charge.

By the time they finished their sandwiches, darkness had started to swallow the skyline and Poppy leaned back against the big oak tree trunk. She could still make out the silhouette of their horses, and she wondered what Crystal would think of their next big adventure, camping out with so many other horses and people for five whole glorious days.

'Want to go into the tent?' she asked, yawning.

Katie immediately shifted beside her. 'Yeah, let's get inside and zip it up.'

Poppy stood and held out a hand for Katie, yanking her to her feet. She didn't even bother to make fun of how nervous her friend was, and for once Milly didn't either.

'I'm still starved,' Milly moaned. 'Did you pack any snacks?'

Poppy laughed. 'Sure did. We have chips and Tim Tams and . . .' She rummaged in her bag. 'And rice crackers.'

Milly grabbed the bag. 'We definitely need to start with the Tim Tams.'

Poppy crawled into the tent, pulling the bag and Milly with her. Katie scooted in behind and quickly zipped it up. Katie turned on a torch, and Milly made funny faces, the light and shadows playing across her features as she started munching her way through the packet of chocolate biscuits.

'Did you hear that?' said Katie, suddenly.

Poppy paused, her hand resting on the almost empty biscuit packet. She stifled a sigh. 'No, Katie. I didn't hear anything.'

Katie's eyes were so wide they reminded Poppy of a balloon about to pop! 'I heard something. A rustling.'

Milly licked her chocolatey fingers as she made a face at Poppy then turned to Katie. 'You're probably right. It could be a possum or a kangaroo or a lizard or . . .'

'Not helping!' Katie muttered.

'Yeah, shut up, Mils,' Poppy said, nudging Milly affectionately. She swiped a biscuit. 'There was no noise, okay?'

She was about to take a bite when . . .

Rustle. Rustle.

'Who's hearing things now?' Katie hissed.

Poppy froze. Her mouth was suddenly dry as she dropped her biscuit and held out her hand to Katie.

Rustle. Rustle.

Something *was* out there!

It was Milly who reached for the torch, holding it between them. No one said anything. Silence stretched endlessly and Poppy strained her ears, wondering if she'd imagined it, wondering if . . .

'Ugggghhhhhhh!' Katie screamed.

A huge shadow loomed outside the tent. Poppy's heart was beating so hard she thought it was going to leap straight out of her chest. A scream locked in her throat as the shadow swiped at the tent.

We're going to die. Something is hunting us. Poppy's mind was screaming out words that never came out of her mouth.

'Arghhhh!' Milly shrieked.

Woof!

'What on earth?' Poppy exclaimed.

Woof! Woof! Woof!

'Casper?' Milly unzipped the tent.

Even though she'd heard the bark, Poppy's heart was still racing, and Katie held her hand so tight she thought it was going to break.

'It could be a dingo come to eat us!' Katie wailed. 'Don't open it!'

But even as she spoke a ball of fur came hurtling into the tent, muddy paws flying over their sleeping-bags, long wet tongue slathering them as Casper leapt around in circles, not seeming to know whom he was most excited about finding.

'Casper!' Poppy scolded, trying to grab his collar and hold him down. 'Naughty boy! You frightened the life out of us!'

'I'm going to kill that dog!' Katie bellowed. 'This is not a game, Casper!'

Milly was laughing, bear hugging Casper and wrangling him to the ground. 'Yuk, he stinks!' she squealed. 'You're so gross, Casper!'

Poppy's heart had finally slowed and she looked over at Katie, her face still pale as a ghost's, and offered a smile. 'I'm sorry he scared you like that,' she said. 'He must have been out looking for us. He's a mess.'

Casper's usually beautiful coat was covered in leaves and grass, and his legs were filthy. He must have stopped for a drink in the creek before surprising them.

'Grab the phone,' Katie said, her voice still shaky but starting to sound more like her normal practical self. 'I wonder how long he's been missing?'

Poppy fumbled for her bag and found her phone, grimacing when she noticed a missed call and two text messages. She'd had it on silent during the ride and totally forgotten all about checking in again with her aunt and uncle. She scanned the first text.

Casper has disappeared. Let us know if you see or hear him.

Poppy swiped down to the next message.

Any sign of Casper? We're getting worried. Please check in before bed.

'Looks like he's been missing a while,' Poppy told the others, elbowing Casper away when he tried to lick her face again. 'Can you give him something to eat? Anyone have some leftover sandwich?'

Poppy replied to Aunt Sophie.

Casper here. He scared us to death scratching outside the tent! We'll keep him zipped in with us for the night.

She put her phone down and reached over to stroke Casper. Better him than a wild fox!

'Come on,' she said. 'Let's snuggle down and go to sleep.' It had been a long day and her eyelids were starting to droop, although Casper was panting so loudly from his adventure that she doubted any of them would be able to sleep for a while yet. 'You're crazy, you know that? Crazy but clever,' she told the dog.

'No way we're sleeping yet!' Milly argued. 'We still have snacks to eat, and besides, there's no one here telling us to go to sleep. We can stay awake all night if we want.'

A slow grin spread across Poppy's face. 'True.' She rubbed at her eyes and reached for a bottle of Sprite she'd tucked into her bag when she'd been packing the food. Maybe the sugar would help her to stay awake. She unscrewed the top and took a big gulp, before passing it to Katie.

'I'm never going to be able to sleep now anyway,' Katie moaned after taking a swig and passing the bottle over to Milly.

'You definitely won't be able to sleep once I'm finished telling my first scary story,' Milly said in a low voice. 'So, one night around a campfire two friends were sitting, listening to the silence . . . when they heard a noise. *Drip, drip, drip*, it went.'

'Noooo.' Katie put her fingers in her ears. 'La-la-la-la, can't hear you.'

Poppy laughed.

'Come on, it's just a story!' Milly protested, holding the torch to her chin and making a ghoulish face.

'La-la-la-la-la-la,' Katie kept on singing. 'La-la-la-la-la.'

Milly had her mouth open wide, eyes crossed, like she was pretending to be a zombie.

'Milly, stop!' Katie demanded.

Poppy sipped more Sprite and snuggled up to Casper. 'Hey, if we don't get eaten alive by anything tonight, we should do this more often next holidays. We could camp at lots of different spots around the farm.'

'Not helping, Pops,' Katie groaned. 'I'm trying to think of us *not* being eaten alive!'

Just then a screeching noise made Poppy's heart stop. She shivered.

'Poppy?' Katie whimpered.

Casper let out a loud *woof* and wagged his tail.

Poppy took a deep breath, knowing she was just unnerved because of Katie. 'It'll just be a bat,' she said. 'Look, give me the torch.'

Her hand was shaking as she took the torch from Milly and bravely unzipped the tent, poking her head out and shining the torch around. She scanned the trees, going from branch to branch, but she couldn't see anything.

'Where is it?' Katie asked.

Poppy gulped, wishing she'd been able to see something to put them all at ease. Just then the noise sounded out again and she shone her torch around wildly.

'There.' Katie's voice sounded as soft as a breath of air. 'There are two bats hanging there. When you see them like that, they're actually really sweet-looking.'

Poppy leaned into her, their heads pressed

together. 'Yeah, they are pretty cute little guys,' she said, as if she'd been so sure all along. 'Let's just put on some music so we can't hear anything else.'

Poppy zipped the tent back, glancing up at the trees one last time.

'Don't tell me you're spooked out now too?' Milly asked. 'I can't babysit both of you.'

Poppy laughed. 'No way. Not me.'

It was only half a lie. Up until a few minutes ago she hadn't been scared of anything!

Casper was snoring loudly now, and Poppy slipped into her sleeping-bag to stay warm, struggling to stretch out her legs with the heavy dog in the way. It was going to be a very, very long night.

Poppy opened her eyes and stretched her arms out before clambering out of her sleeping-bag and quietly unzipping the tent. The others were snoring still and she left them to sleep; they'd talked and eaten way too much until late into the night. She rubbed her eyes when she poked her head out, the sunlight bright. Spring was her favourite time of year, especially the lovely mornings when it was so close to being summer and the sun shone high from early in the day.

She climbed out and Casper pushed past her eagerly and ran over to the ponies. Crystal was standing with Cody, patiently waiting behind the tape. She grinned and gave her pony a little wave. It was so cool waking up and having Crystal right there.

Six more sleeps until we'll be doing this every day!

She turned to go back into the tent then quickly spun back around. Wait a minute: there were only *two* horses standing on the other side of the temporary fence.

She rubbed at her eyes again and stared, her heart pounding as she frantically scanned for another horse.

'Milly, wake up!' she yelled, frozen like a statue as she kept her eyes locked on the horses. 'We've lost Joe!'

How could they have lost a horse? Where could he have gone between them falling asleep and waking up?

'Milly!'

'What?' Milly burst out of the tent, her hair a halo of wild curls around her. 'What do you meant we've lost him?'

Katie emerged behind her, a hair tie between her teeth as she scooped her long hair back into a ponytail.

'I mean that he's gone,' Poppy said. 'He must've escaped during the night.'

Milly was immobile for a second, clearly in shock, before tearing off in just her socks towards the creek.

'Milly, come back. We'll all go looking for him.'

'Nooooo!' Milly wailed. 'Joe! Joe!' she yelled. 'Joe, where are you?'

Poppy traded looks with Katie, trying to stay calm. 'Do you think we should pack up first, or just go looking for him?'

Katie shrugged. 'I don't know. But we might start looking for him and find out he's made his way home, so maybe packing up here properly first would be best?'

Poppy agreed. 'Come on, let's do it quickly before she freaks out even more.'

Casper appeared, wagging his tail. He shook

and sprayed Poppy with water. 'Ew!' she squealed. 'Get away!' Casper woofed and danced on the spot, tail whipping back and forth behind him. 'Casper!'

'We need to go!' Milly announced as she ran back toward them, pushing past the dog, hands on her hips. 'He could be anywhere by now!'

'Milly, calm down,' Poppy said, planting her hands on her friend's shoulders. 'He escaped, he wasn't stolen, so it's just a matter of finding him and catching him. He's on the property somewhere. Everything's going to be okay.' Or at least, she hoped it was.

Milly's eyes were wild. 'I hadn't even thought about him being *stolen*! What if someone took him? *Ohmygod,* what if he's gone forever?'

She began dancing around on the spot, pulling her boots on.

'Milly, we're going to pack up so we can look for him properly,' Poppy said soothingly. She ducked into the tent and rolled up the sleeping-bags with Katie, stuffing them into their bags and packing up all the chip and biscuit wrappers.

'He's probably grazing nearby,' she said loudly. 'He's so sneaky getting out like that.'

Katie laughed. 'It's weird the other two didn't try to follow him.'

'Come on, you two! Hurry up!' Milly shoved the side of the tent impatiently and it collapsed on them. Poppy overbalanced and landed on Katie.

'Milly!' she screamed out.

'Did she seriously just do that to us?' Katie muttered. 'I say we let her go find her own stinking horse.'

Poppy giggled and crawled out of the deflated tent. 'You do realise you've just slowed us down, right?' she said to Milly. It's kind of impossible to get everything out of here now! Help us!'

Milly grumbled and bent in to help haul Katie out.

Just as Katie was about to scold Milly, Crystal let out an ear-piercing whinny and Poppy looked up.

'He's there!' she cried, shielding her eyes from the bright morning sun. 'Joe's just over there!'

Joe was grazing on some long grass near the edge of the trees, but when he looked up and saw Milly coming towards him, he lifted his tail high and pranced off, quickly disappearing.

'He's so naughty,' Katie said, passing Poppy the

bag for the tent. Poppy held it open as Katie put some things in and then folded the tent up. She was seriously fast at dismantling it, almost quicker than when she'd put it up. 'We'll be chasing him all day.'

Just then Milly came back, panting and doubled over. 'Can you remind me how much I hate that little rat when we catch up with him?'

Poppy sighed. So much for hanging out a bit longer and having breakfast like they'd planned. 'Come on, let's go,' she said. 'Mils, you can ride double with me. And you owe us. Big time.'

'Yeah, I know,' Milly grumbled. 'Can we just get going?'

Poppy hefted up her saddle and passed it to Milly. 'Here. You get Crystal ready and I'll finish up with this stuff. But I think we should leave it all here now we know he's close by, don't you? We have to leave Milly's saddle anyway as there's no way we can carry everything between two horses.'

'Do you think we have any chance of catching him?' Katie asked Poppy in a low voice as Milly rushed over to wrap the fence tape up.

Poppy shrugged. 'No idea. I'd say we have more chance of running him back home than actually grabbing hold of him, but I guess we'll see.'

Finally they were ready, with Milly on Crystal's back behind Poppy. Milly shuffled close to her, arms looped around her waist, and when Katie signalled she was ready, they walked off in search of the elusive pony.

'There he is!' Katie exclaimed after five minutes. 'Look, he's right behind those trees, I can see his bum sticking out.'

Poppy squinted at where Katie was pointing. Joe was grazing happily on his own, completely unaware that he'd caused such a commotion.

'Let's walk over really quietly,' whispered Poppy.

But she'd totally forgotten about Casper.

With a loud bark he ran off ahead of them, ruining their element of surprise.

Joe watched them coming nearer, and as Milly squeezed Poppy tighter around the waist, just when they were almost close enough to him, he snorted and trotted off.

'I'm going to kill him!' Milly grumbled. 'Why is he so naughty?!'

Poppy sighed and nudged Crystal on with her heels. It was going to be a very, very long morning.

They followed Joe for what felt like forever until he eventually dipped his head to graze again.

'Let's just keep walking. Ignore him completely,' Poppy suggested. 'Kind of like when I was trying to train Storm.'

When she'd started out with her brumby, she'd ignored him until he'd finally come to her on his own terms. Maybe the same would work with Joe.

Milly nodded and Poppy led the way, giving Joe a wide berth and then walking around him. They kept going, and she grinned when she glanced back and saw that he was watching them.

He hesitated, and then *he* began following *them*.

'You're a genius,' Milly declared. 'An absolute horse-whispering genius.'

'Do we keep going or stop?' Katie whispered, moving Cody next to them.

'Let's stop,' Poppy suggested. 'Milly, if he comes close, why don't you slide your leg over so you're sitting side saddle on Crystal's bottom facing him. Then you can slip down and grab him when the time is right. We're lucky he still has his halter on.'

'Okay,' said Milly.

They waited, not turning to look at Joe. Poppy let her reins slide through her fingers so Crystal could snack at some grass. From the corner of her eye, she watched Joe move closer and closer. Finally she elbowed Milly.

'Now,' she murmured.

Milly wriggled around behind her and Poppy held her breath, hoping, waiting . . .

Oomph!

Crystal let rip a whopping great buck, and Poppy madly scrambled to keep her balance and pick up the reins.

'Help!' Milly hollered, flying off Crystal and landing with a thud.

'Crystal!' Poppy scolded, trying to steady herself with her stupidly big pack pulling her off-balance. She pulled Crystal up sharply to stop the pony from trampling her friend.

'Got him!' Katie announced.

Milly and Poppy looked up, disorientated. Katie was hanging off Cody, clutching Joe's halter.

'Amazing,' Poppy giggled. 'I thought we'd lost him for sure that time!'

Milly stomped off and quickly clipped her lead

rope to Joe's halter, and Poppy watched as she glared at Joe and gave him a telling off.

'We are so not friends now,' Milly scolded Joe, tying the rope to the other side of his halter to make reins and then throwing it over his head.

Her chestnut pony had his ears pricked, nostrils flared, looking very happy with himself for escaping and then playing such a fun game.

'Now I have to ride you back to get your saddle and bridle.'

'Hey, at least we found him and he wasn't injured or anything,' Poppy said, trying to make Milly feel better.

'Yeah, I guess,' Milly said, frowning as she rode up beside Poppy and Katie. 'I'm really sorry he ruined our morning.'

Poppy shrugged. 'You'd do the same for us. I'm sorry Crystal bucked you off like that.'

Milly grimaced and rubbed her sore backside and they all laughed.

They rode back toward their campsite. Poppy hated that the weekend was almost over now – by the time they got back and did their chores, it would be time to head home. Then again, the sooner they got home, the closer it would be to their five days away at Barmah National Park, and she couldn't wait for that.

As long as none of their ponies escaped when they were at Barmah, because finding them in that forest would be a disaster!

CHAPTER FIVE

Let's Go

Poppy stood up to do her speech. She couldn't believe that her mum was coming to pick her up from school in less than an hour. She glanced at the clock on the wall. Again. It had only been five days since their camping night, but it felt like forever ago.

Her teacher was letting her do her speech first, since she was leaving early, and her stomach danced with nerves.

'Brumbies are not . . .'

She stumbled to a halt as Lukas mumbled something to Ryder, raising his eyebrows and laughing. She cleared her throat, fixing her gaze on her best friend, Sarah. Sarah smiled and she smiled back, wishing she were better at talking in front of her class.

'Brumbies are not native to Australia,' she said, starting again in a louder, more confident voice. 'They are heritage horses that descended from the first horses that came to Australia on ships from England and either escaped or were released. Over the years they have adjusted genetically to thrive in the wild. It is believed they share Thoroughbred, Arabian, Draft and Clydesdale bloodlines.' Poppy cleared her throat. 'Our largest brumby populations live in the Northern Territory, Queensland and northern Western Australia, but we also have brumbies in Victoria and New South Wales, and the Australian wild horse population is now over one million.'

The boys nudged each other again, but Poppy stayed focused on Sarah, pretending she was only talking to her. 'Water is the biggest threat to the brumby, because even in areas where feed is plentiful, many of them die during periods of drought. Different states in Australia have different views on how to manage brumbies, and although many people love our heritage horse, the brumby is considered a feral pest by the government and environmental groups. But anyone who has worked with a brumby knows what amazing animals they are to train and work with, as well as being perfectly suited to the Australian climate and conditions.'

She finished and the class clapped. Many of them began studying the images she'd passed around and talking eagerly about them.

'That was a wonderful, informative speech, Poppy. Thank you for sharing with us something you're obviously so passionate about,' said Ms Vincent. 'On the topic of sharing, is there something you'd like to share back there, Ryder?'

Ryder shook his head.

'Perhaps a question for Poppy?'

'I don't get why she cares so much. Why not let them all get killed?' Ryder asked.

'Yeah, it seems like everyone else on the planet thinks they're pests anyway,' said Lukas.

Poppy's cheeks burned and she plopped down in her chair beside Sarah.

'Poppy has a beautiful brumby of her own. I bet you wouldn't say that if you'd seen him,' Sarah snapped back.

'Doubt it.'

'Enough! Stay behind to talk to me after class,' the teacher said, pointing to the boys. 'And Poppy, have a wonderful week riding. The rest of us can't wait to hear about your brumby adventures at Barmah.'

Poppy looked at the clock, her face so hot and flushed she thought she might be sick. Why were boys so stupid? Well, not all boys. Her little brother was fun – most of the time.

'They're so dumb,' Kim said, rolling her eyes. 'Don't listen to them. Brumbies sound amazing.' The other girls nodded.

Poppy smiled. They were right. And if the boys had been mean to her about anything else, she wouldn't have even cared, but brumbies meant a lot to her and she hated anyone saying they should be killed.

'Go and have fun,' Sarah whispered, pointing at the clock, and Poppy bent to give her a quick hug. She grabbed her bag, waved to her other friends and darted out of the classroom. She ran through the school, skidding to a stop outside the office and ducking in to sign herself out. She smiled at the office lady as she tapped in her details, then bolted out the door and ran down to her mum's car. She was breathless when she yanked open the door and dropped into the passenger seat.

'Thanks, Mum,' Poppy panted, knowing how difficult it was for her to leave work and drive over to get her.

'All day I've been looking forward to spending some time, just the two of us,' her mum said, smiling over at her.

Poppy's stomach growled. Loudly. She reached for her schoolbag and pulled out her lunch box to see what she still had left.

'You hungry?'

'Yes,' Poppy moaned.

'That's lucky. I thought we'd stop at a café on the way, have a juice and something to eat. What do you say?'

Poppy dropped her lunch box and grinned. 'Sounds great.'

It wasn't until they were both sitting by the window in the sun, drinking juices and eating cupcakes, that Poppy realised something was up. Her mum had a strange look on her face – the kind of look that reminded Poppy of when her mum had tried to break the news to her that her dad had died.

Poppy fiddled with the sugar packets on the table. 'What is it?' she asked.

Her mum sighed and took a sip of her juice. 'Poppy, I've been trying to figure out the best way to tell you this,' she said, 'but . . .'

Poppy gulped and waited. 'What is it?'

'Well . . .' She paused again. She looked nervous. 'Poppy I've met someone. A lovely man through work. We've been out a few times when you've been at Starlight and your brother's been at a sleepover. And for lunch here and there. He's really nice. I think when you get back you should meet him.'

Poppy's lips were frozen around her straw. She could barely breathe.

'He's just love– '

'Lovely,' Poppy finished for her, finally finding her voice again. 'Yup, I caught that the first time.'

Her mother's face flushed. Poppy forced down some juice, then she reached for her fork and started stabbing at her cupcake and eating chunks of it. How could her mum have a boyfriend? Her dad had only been gone a year!

'I didn't mean to meet anyone so soon, Pops,' her mum said, as if she could suddenly read Poppy's mind. 'But he's a great guy and he makes me laugh. I really hoped you'd be grown up enough to understand that.'

Poppy stared down at her cupcake, at the pink frosting that had looked so pretty, but tasted like cardboard. She took a deep breath and finally brought her eyes up to meet her mum's. Poppy could see how hopeful she looked, how happy.

'Do you still love Dad?' Poppy asked, her voice all croaky.

'Yes! Of course I love your dad still,' her mum said, tears welling in her eyes. 'I will never love anyone like I love your dad and you and your brother. But I'd really like to think that your father would want me to be happy. All of us.'

'It's just … I don't know. It's weird,' Poppy whispered. 'And yeah, of course Dad would want you to be happy. I just don't think I want to meet him.' What would her brother think? Surely Tom wouldn't want to meet the guy either?

Her mum took her hand. 'That's fine, Poppy. Whenever you're ready, you just tell me.'

'Does Tom know?' she asked.

Her mum shook her head. 'No, sweetheart. I wanted to talk to you about it first.'

'Don't tell him,' she blurted, suddenly worried about Tom finding out without her being there. 'Can you wait until I'm back? I think it'd be weird for him and I just . . .' She blinked away tears. Since their dad had died, she'd always looked out for Tom and made sure he was okay. She wanted to be with him now. 'Just please wait.'

'Of course,' her mum said, and Poppy saw there were tears in her eyes too. 'I'll wait until you're home and we can all talk about it together.'

They ate their cupcakes in silence then, until her mum started asking her about the big ride and Poppy started telling her about the stupid boys in her class, and how much she was looking forward to brumby spotting. The idea of her mum hanging out with another man who wasn't her dad felt like there was a fly in her brain that she was constantly swatting away. She was going to try not to think about it. Not just yet, anyway.

'Girls, have you packed all your stuff in the truck?'
Aunt Sophie's voice echoed through the stables.

'We're all packed!' Poppy called back.
'Everything's in except our packs. They're up at the
house still.'

She mentally went through everything – saddle,
bridle, cover, grooming and first-aid kits, buckets,
haybales, tents, sleeping-bags. She was sure that
was all they needed. She'd put fresh straw in the
stables after Milly and Katie had mucked them out,
and before that they'd taken all the horses out to
the paddocks so they could graze while they were
away. The only horses housed inside tonight were
the ones going on the big ride tomorrow.

'Hey,' Poppy said, hearing a kicking noise and
turning to look at Storm. He was fretting in his
stable, kicking at the timber sidewall, and when he
poked his head over the half-door, she could see his
eyes were wide.

'You're okay,' she told him, going down to get
him some more hay and then letting herself into his
stall. 'It's just a bit of rain on the roof – nothing to
be frightened of.' It was funny how much he loved a
storm if he was outside in it, but acted like a scared

child when he was locked in. The rain was loud on the tin above, and because he hadn't yet spent a lot of time indoors, Poppy wondered if that was why it was extra spooky. 'Have something to eat and you'll feel better.'

Her own stomach was growling; she hadn't eaten anything since the cupcake with her mum.

'Let's head up for dinner, then early to bed,' Aunt Sophie said as she walked through the stable block.

Poppy gave Storm a lingering pat and let herself out, careful to lock his door.

'Everyone who's in for the night has fresh water?' asked Aunt Sophie.

Poppy nodded. 'Yes. I've double-checked them.'

Milly and Katie appeared and they all walked to the door. The rain was starting to fall heavily, and Poppy hoped it wouldn't ruin their trail ride.

'I'm making a run for it!' Katie squealed.

Poppy sprinted off with her, the cool lash of rain against her bare arms sending chills through her body. She laughed when Milly hoofed it past them – no matter how hard she tried, Poppy could never catch her.

Finally they reached the house and Poppy kicked off her boots and leapt inside, skidding on the timber floor in her socks and following her nose into the kitchen. Aunt Sophie must have had something in the slow cooker, because the whole place smelt amazing.

An hour later they'd eaten dinner, done the dishes and were upstairs getting ready for bed. Poppy flopped back and buried herself under the covers, squeezing her eyes shut tight. She listened to Milly and Katie chatting and then she felt the indent of weight on her bed.

'Poppy, is something wrong? You've been really quiet,' Katie said.

Poppy bit down hard on her lip as a hot burst of tears filled her eyes. She hadn't expected them to notice.

'Poppy?' Milly asked.

Poppy took a deep breath. She'd been trying not to think about it since she'd gotten on the train, and then she'd distracted herself all evening with the horses, but it came back like a flood now.

'My mum has a boyfriend,' she whispered.

There was silence, and then she felt a hand on her arm. She looked up and into Milly's eyes.

'That sucks,' Milly said, frowning. 'I mean, that *really* sucks.'

'What's he like?' Katie asked. 'Did your mum tell you or did you find out?'

Poppy pushed herself up and sat up against the wall. She brushed her tears away with the back of her hand. 'She told me before she dropped me at the train station today,' she said. 'I just . . .' Poppy struggled to find the right words.

'You still wish your dad would come home,' Katie said in a low voice. 'I can't imagine my mum or dad being with anyone else.'

'Have you met him?' Milly asked.

Poppy shook her head. 'Nope. I told her I don't want to. And yeah, it's so weird. I just don't want to see mum with anyone else. I can still imagine Dad being there, coming home and us going back to how it used to be. I miss him so bad sometimes.'

'You know . . .' Katie hesitated. 'Maybe it's hard for your mum. I mean, she has you guys, but you spend heaps of time here and it sounds like Tom has lots of friends. It's probably kind of lonely for her. Does she seem happy?'

Poppy wrapped her arms tightly around herself. She had never thought about her mum feeling lonely, even when she was depressed, but she did seem so much happier now she'd found someone. Maybe Katie was right: Poppy had Starlight Stables, Crystal and Storm, plus she was always hanging out with Milly and Katie on the weekends and Sarah when she was at home.

'She does kind of have a point,' Milly said. 'But it still sucks.'

Poppy glanced at Katie and smiled. 'I guess I hadn't thought about how she feels. Thanks.'

They all sat in silence for a while. Poppy didn't want to talk about it any more – her eyes were burning – and they probably didn't know what else to say anyway.

'Want us never to talk about it again?' Milly asked.

Poppy laughed through her tears at Milly's overly arched eyebrows and overly serious face. 'Yeah, actually that'd be kind of great if you could do that.'

Milly gave her a little salute and Katie smiled, and Poppy realised she was happy she'd told them. It made the whole thing less scary somehow.

'Lights out?' Aunt Sophie's soft voice made Poppy turn. She was standing in the doorway.

'Night, Aunt Sophie,' Poppy said, hoping she hadn't heard what they'd been talking about.

'Goodnight,' Milly and Katie said at the same time.

Poppy breathed deep in the sudden darkness. They were leaving early in the morning, and she was so tired she couldn't keep her eyes open for a second longer.

Poppy loaded Crystal into the trailer, and once she'd secured the gate behind the pony's bottom and tied her up, she took Storm from her aunt so she could lead him on. He snorted at the ramp and stamped his hoof once, and Poppy was sure he was going to baulk and pull away. She held the lead rope firmly.

'Walk on,' she instructed sternly.

He stood for a moment, then placidly walked on, his head dipped down like it was the most normal thing in the world to be doing on a Saturday morning. She couldn't believe it!

'Good boy,' she praised, ducking under the breast bar at the front and tying him up beside Crystal. It was amazing how different he was now, almost like he'd never been a wild horse. Aunt Sophie had done such an amazing job of training him.

Poppy waited until Sophie had put the tailgate up and then ducked out the side door. 'See you guys soon!' she said, closing the door and double-checking it had locked. She clapped her hands together to get rid of the dust and then surveyed the scene in front of her.

Aunt Sophie had decided to let Crystal and Storm travel together since they were friends, and Crystal would hopefully keep him nice and calm. Cody, Joe and Uncle Mark's horse, Shadow, were loaded on the truck, which could barely fit them all along with the camping gear.

'Let's go, girls!' Uncle Mark ordered, pointing to the vehicle. 'Who's in here with me, and who's in the truck with Sophie?'

Poppy glanced at her friends. Were they

thinking the same as her? That they should all travel up together?

'Ah, take them all,' Aunt Sophie said with a laugh. 'I'm fine on my own and it'll be more fun for them that way.'

Poppy threw her aunt a grin and ran to Mark's vehicle. 'Shot gun!' she called out, diving in and buckling up before anyone could challenge her.

'So not fair!' Milly moaned, climbing in the back with Katie.

Poppy looked out at Casper, behind the fence in his run. He didn't get left out of the fun very often – he was usually in the house with everyone else and sneaking onto beds to sleep, and he looked sad. But it was only for a few days, and he wasn't allowed in the National Park. Her aunt and uncle had someone coming in twice a day to check the other horses and take Casper out for a run.

Sophie rumbled on ahead of them, and Uncle Mark slowly pulled out and followed her across the field and down onto their driveway. They bumped across the gravel, and Poppy twisted in her seat to look back, just able to make out her horses' faces through the window in the trailer.

'Settle in for a long drive, girls,' Uncle Mark said. 'We should be there in about two and a half hours, depending on the traffic.'

Poppy wriggled back in her seat and stared out the window at gum trees and fences, fields full of cattle and then horses. A sign whizzed past.

She sat on her hands and tried not to jiggle in her seat, a big grin spreading across her face that she couldn't stop.

No more sleeps, she whispered to herself. *Barmah National Park, here we come!*

CHAPTER SIX

Ready, Set, Camp!

'Getting excited yet?' Uncle Mark asked.

Poppy looked out the window as the vehicle slowed and her uncle turned into the entrance of Barmah National Park. The sign to their left was weathered, but Poppy scanned it as they passed.

'More like *dying* of excitement,' Milly said from behind her.

'I just can't believe we're here,' Poppy said, putting her window down and leaning out a little. The wind brushed her cheeks and she stared at the towering trees.

'Those trees are huge,' Katie said as they drove deeper into the forest, following Sophie's truck.

Poppy put her window up as they made their way up the dusty drive. 'I can't remember what they're called.'

'River red gums,' Uncle Mark clarified. 'And we have to be careful of them because they shed branches without warning.'

'Thanks for the FYI,' Milly muttered. 'I'll make sure not to put my tent under one!'

Poppy laughed. 'I think we're camping in the old muster yards, aren't we?'

'We sure are,' Uncle Mark replied.

Poppy had read all about it. If they were here without their horses and just camping, they'd be camping somewhere along the Murray River. They'd definitely have to be careful of the trees if they ever did that. But as part of the organised heritage ride they got to stay in the historic muster yards.

They eventually came to a stop and Poppy couldn't believe how many people were already there.

Trucks and horse trailers were all parked in lines, and people were leading horses and milling about. It was just like at the last competition they'd been to – only then, the horses had been groomed to within an inch of their life and all the riders were wearing fancy jackets and velvet helmets. Here, the horses looked more relaxed, and everyone was wearing normal clothes.

'What do you think?' Katie asked as they all stepped out of the vehicle.

Poppy smiled as she surveyed the scene in front of her. She could just make out a barbecue set up past the line of trucks, where smoke rose in the air, and she turned and grabbed her friends' hands, squeezing them tight.

'This is going to be the best trip ever!'

Uncle Mark gestured for them to help and Poppy quickly opened the side door of the trailer to check on her two horses.

Katie and Milly disappeared, but Poppy didn't see them go. She was too busy fussing over Crystal and Storm.

A heaving, creaking noise signalled that Mark was putting the back ramp down, and she undid Storm's rope and stroked his neck. He snorted and stamped his hoof, impatient to get out of the confined space.

'I'm going to take Storm off first,' she called out.

'Ready when you are,' said Uncle Mark as the small gate behind Storm's rump opened and Poppy ushered him off. He was in a hurry and raced backwards, but she managed to keep him straight, and when he was off the ramp he let out a loud whinny, dancing in a circle as he surveyed their new surroundings. He was holding his head so high in the air she burst out laughing.

'Look at you! You've grown another hand high!'

His dark, almost-black coat gleamed in the sunlight, and Poppy could imagine him at a show. He looked every bit as amazing as any of the other horses she'd seen at competitions and she grinned when she saw some riders standing back to admire him.

'Someone's excited,' Uncle Mark said.

Poppy stroked his neck. It was thick and hard with muscle as he stayed all tensed up.

'Do you think he knows where he is?' Poppy asked.

Mark shrugged and took the rope from her. 'Horses remember a lot more than we give them credit for.'

Poppy left Storm with Mark and unloaded Crystal on her own, always surprised by how quietly she walked off the ramp, patiently waiting for Poppy to show her where they were going.

'Where do you think we take them?' Poppy asked, holding both ponies for a moment while Mark secured the ramp and bolted it.

'Let's go find the others and follow them.'

Poppy led Crystal and watched as Storm stepped fast beside Uncle Mark, head still high, nostrils flared.

She was certain he knew it was his old home, and she wondered if he was recognising smells. Was he remembering his old mob?

'This is so cool,' Milly said, falling into step beside her and leading a very excited, prancing Joe. 'I can't believe we're here.'

Cody trotted sedately behind them, behaving perfectly as always.

'Sausages! Secure your horses then come and have something to eat!' yelled a woman waving from behind the barbecue.

Poppy's mouth watered. She slowed to read a sign.

No dogs permitted in the muster yards.

Members & registered riders only.

Red ribbons on tails for stallions & horses who kick.

One horse length between each rider at all times.

She made a mental note to keep an eye out for those red ribbons as they neared some yards. A lady holding a clipboard was waiting at the entrance.

'These are the temporary yards where the horses are to be kept,' the woman said to Aunt Sophie.

'You all right with both of them, Pops?' Uncle Mark asked. 'I'm going to get their water sorted and fetch some hay from the truck.'

Poppy nodded and took Storm's lead rope. He'd calmed down a little, but he was still looking around, ears pricked as he surveyed the scene. She held both ropes tightly, one horse on each side of her, and waited for Aunt Sophie to finish talking to the lady.

It felt nice having both of them beside her. She was so proud of Storm and she loved him so much, but she wondered if he was confused when he saw her with Crystal all the time. She loved having two horses, but she hated sometimes having to choose between them.

'Hi, girls!' the woman said brightly as Sophie led Shadow into the yards. 'We're going to have a great few days here at Barmah.'

Poppy nodded and smiled as they passed. The forest smelt amazing, and she was so happy the rain had stopped. But everything felt fresh and vibrant because of it; droplets of water still twinkled on some of the leaves and the ground wasn't too dusty.

'Over here, girls,' called Aunt Sophie. She'd put Shadow into his makeshift yard, and now she took Storm.

Poppy secured Crystal and unclipped her lead rope, watching as all the horses moved about and inspected their new surroundings. Uncle Mark came back lugging water and Poppy turned to him.

'We'll get the hay,' she suggested.

He nodded and the three friends walked back toward the truck, chatting excitedly.

'This is so cool. Check out all the horses that are here already,' Katie hissed.

'I know. Do you think a lot of them are brumbies?' Poppy asked. There seemed to be all types of horses and ponies – big draft horses, finer-boned Thoroughbreds and then a whole lot of cross-breed types. She guessed some of them could have been brumbies, but she wasn't sure.

A girl walked past them then and Poppy turned back to look at her. She looked familiar, but Poppy couldn't work out where she'd seen her. Maybe it was at a competition?

'*Oh. My. God,*' Milly exclaimed.

'What?' Poppy asked.

'That was Sienna Andrews,' Milly gasped. 'I can't believe you didn't recognise her!'

'Do you think we'll be riding with her?' Katie asked, eyes wide as she met Poppy's gaze.

Sienna Andrews. Poppy racked her brain and then it hit her. 'Did she win the Australian Brumby Challenge?'

'Duh.' Milly laughed. 'I could have told you that the second she walked past us!'

Poppy looked back, trying to see Sienna's long, almost-black hair, but she'd disappeared. Now she remembered reading all about the riding star in a *HorseWyse* magazine that Katie had brought to the farm one weekend. She was the youngest ever trainer to win, only eighteen years old, and the fact that she was a girl made it even cooler.

'Come on, let's get this hay and help set up camp so we can explore!' Milly jumped up into the truck and Poppy followed her, eager to get back to the horses and find out what they'd be doing next.

It was amazing. Poppy looked around, trying to stop her jaw from hanging open. The yards were so old they felt almost haunted, the timber faded and worn and huge trees brushing against the top rail in the far corner. A shiver ran through Poppy as she gazed up to the tallest tree, its gnarled trunk twisting so high in the air that she wondered if it was as ancient as the yards.

'This is a special and historic moment,' the woman speaking announced, sitting atop one of the upper rails of the large yards. 'This yard was built in the 1800s. It's hard to believe it's been here so long. Back then, Barmah was used as winter grazing for cattle, and riders would gather to bring them into the very yards you're standing in.'

Poppy looked over at Katie and Milly and saw

that they were both as entranced as her. It was even more incredible than she'd imagined. The cattle yards looked so different to the pictures she'd seen. In real life they were magical, and she loved that they'd been used so many years ago for big cattle musters.

'We're allowed one hundred riders per day here, so please check the schedules and make sure you know what times and days you'll be riding. And kids, make sure your parent or guardian is riding with you at all times.'

'I just imagined my mum was here riding with me,' Milly said with a giggle. *'Oh darling, where are the showers!? It's awfully dusty and smelly out here, Amelia.'*

Katie leaned into Poppy helplessly as they broke into peals of laughter.

'You're so mean,' Poppy said when she'd finally caught her breath. 'I bet your mum doesn't sound like that.'

Katie snorted. 'Yeah, she does kind of sound like that.'

Poppy pushed her away playfully. She didn't know the other girls' mums very well, but whenever

Milly's mother dropped her off at Starlight Stables she was dressed in beautiful white outfits and gleaming black heels. Poppy could imagine camping would be very low on her list of Things to Do.

'Come on, let's get something to eat.'

There were a group of helpers back at the barbecue and they waited in line before getting their sausages in bread, plus extras for Sophie and Mark, and slathering them in tomato sauce. They made their way slowly back to where their tent was pitched and Poppy inhaled the smell of horses and forest. She guessed some people would hate it, but she loved it.

'Girls, come and meet Penny Foster,' Aunt Sophie called out, waving them over. They were sitting with an older woman with grey hair, sipping beer and laughing about something.

'Hi,' Poppy said, wandering over and smiling briefly before hurriedly licking the tomato sauce that was starting to drip down her fingers. She passed one of the hotdogs over to her aunt.

'Girls, Penny here is the president of the Victorian Brumby Association. We have her to thank for putting this event on, and for helping to save our beautiful wild horses from slaughter.'

Penny waved at Aunt Sophie as if she was trying to brush away her words. 'Stop trying to make me sound so important.'

'Well, you are,' Uncle Mark said. 'Girls, when people were petitioning to kill the brumbies here, it was Penny who fought to stop them.'

'My brumby actually came from here,' Poppy said, suddenly far more interested in this woman than her food. 'We're not sure what exactly happened to him in the time between when we bought him at auction and now, but we've been told he was one of a handful of brumbies that ended up fleeing the forest during a fire.'

'Ah, so you're the young brumby rescuer,' Penny said, her smile broad. 'I'm impressed with the way you managed to talk your aunt and uncle into saving him with you.'

'I wouldn't say "talked" so much as we had no other option,' Aunt Sophie said wryly.

They all laughed and Poppy felt her cheeks getting hot.

'You know, Poppy, sometimes rescuing one brumby is enough to spur others into action,' Penny said, putting down her drink and getting to her feet. 'The more young people are prepared to challenge the government and stand up for our heritage horses, the better. And with that, I'd better go check everything's ready for tomorrow.'

As she was turning away, Poppy sucked back a breath. 'Does it break your heart when you hear them called feral pests?' she asked, her voice wobbling.

Penny turned and stepped back toward Poppy, reaching for her hand and clasping it tight. 'Yes, my love, it does. These majestic, beautiful creatures have lived on this land for generations and they should be recognised for how special they are.'

Poppy beamed back at her. 'It was lovely to meet you,' she said.

Penny patted her on the shoulder and strode away. She had only gone a couple of metres before she turned back. 'Be sure to find me in the morning, Poppy. You and your friends can ride up front with me and I'll tell you all about the Barmah brumbies.' She waved and disappeared into the crowd.

Poppy spun around to her friends, fists clenched in excitement. 'Did you hear that?' she said slowly.

'Nice work, Pops!' Milly crowed.

'Come on, let's check the horses, get something else to eat and then unpack,' Katie said, looping her arm through Poppy's. 'I want to make sure we're awake early to get that spot with her up front!'

'What a generous offer, girls. Now, make sure you're back before it gets dark,' Aunt Sophie said.

The light was fading fast, the sky tinged with pink as night began to close in. The muster yards were full of all different kinds of tents, and there were small groups of people scattered around, eating dinner and talking. Barbecue smoke and low chatter filtered through the trees and the odd neigh from a horse echoed through the yards.

'I just love camping,' Poppy said in a low voice. 'This is so cool.'

'I know, it's amazing,' Milly replied.

Katie leaned into her and they stood for a moment, taking in the scene before heading toward the horses.

Poppy ducked under the temporary fence to Crystal first, pleased to see that the horses had all settled now and were happily munching their hay. She ran a hand down Crystal's face and absently played with her forelock a moment, twisting the hair as Crystal watched.

'Goodnight,' she whispered, giving her a hug.

Storm lifted his head as she headed his way and let out a little nicker. He was shifting his weight from hoof to hoof and pawing at the ground, and his head was held high, as if he could see something no one else could. Poppy wondered all over again whether he secretly knew where he was and was itching to gallop off and explore the land he'd grown up on as a young colt.

Poppy leaned into him, her nose against his silky neck. She stroked his inky-dark fur and breathed in the scent of him, eyes shut as she leaned against his warmth. Nothing about adopting Storm had been easy, but she'd done the right thing. She smiled. Saving his life had been worth it, even if she was going to have to walk dogs and do chores for the rest of her life to pay for his keep.

CHAPTER SEVEN

Riding Out

There was a sense of excitement as the riders and horses gathered. The morning air was tinged cool, and Poppy snuggled deeper into her hoodie as they waited for everyone to mount. She held her reins on the buckle and sat in her saddle, looking around at the thirty or so horses and riders preparing to ride together. Bits clinked as the horses fidgeted, and some were snorting and stamping their hooves, impatient at having to wait. Poppy slid one hand down Crystal's warm neck. She was alert, with her ears pricked and head held high, but she was standing perfectly still.

Poppy glanced back at Aunt Sophie and was

pleased to see that Storm looked calm but alert, his ears pricked forward like Crystal's. She wished she were riding beside him so she could see him in action, but she couldn't say no to riding up front.

'Can we just get going already?' Milly muttered.

'Shh,' Katie hissed.

Poppy was ready to get going too, but she stayed quiet and waited, and within minutes they were being told to gather up their reins and go. Penny motioned for her to come to the front with a warm smile and Poppy moved up beside her on the wide track. She looked back and saw that Milly and Katie were riding two abreast one horse-length behind.

When Penny spoke, she talked loud enough so many of the riders behind could hear, but there were other guides spread throughout the riders too.

'The land we're riding now was once simply called the Barmah Forest, and it was used for logging and grazing cattle. The majestic Clydesdales were the workhorses of choice at the time, and they were used to log out the red gums, and then during winter, the forest was a winter pasture for those same horses.'

Poppy looked around at the huge tree trunks

and native plants, and watched as a mist rose from the damp forest floor. She looked up towards the blue sky above, tree branches waving lightly in the breeze. When she looked through the towering tree trunks, she could almost see those big Clydesdales hefting big logs behind them, their muscled shoulders gleaming with sweat.

'During World War Two, most of the men were away, and so the horses were left to run wild for years. There was also a large Standardbred horse stud nearby, and they also used the forest over winter to turn out their breeding horses. Even though the horses were rounded up again in spring, there were some who were never brought in and many wild-born foals remained. The mixture of Clydesdale and Standardbred blood is the foundation of the Barmah brumbies that we have grown to love, and it's why they're such hardy, striking horses.'

'So they were just left all alone?' Milly asked, calling out from behind.

'Horses were used for a purpose back then, they were work animals, and even though it might seem that they weren't treated as well as we look after our horses now, most owners rested them properly over winter. Those horses were free to roam the forest as they pleased and had ample shelter and food.'

Poppy gazed around, her hand slipping down to stroke Crystal's neck. Those horses had probably loved being turned out for winter, but it must have been so hard for the ones that spent years away from humans and then were suddenly brought in. She gulped. And even harder for the wild ones who'd never, ever seen a human before and then were captured.

'So is that why so many of the Barmah brumbies have white markings, because of their Clydesdale heritage?' Katie asked.

'Clever girl,' Penny said, laughing. 'That's exactly right. It's also part of the reason many of them have a solid bone structure, with nice big feet and such calm temperaments.'

'So why do so many people want them gone from here?' Poppy asked. 'Are they doing that much damage? I mean, how many even live here?'

'Poppy, the truth is that some people believe they're a pest because of the native plants they could be trampling. And those same people say there are three hundred horses living in this forest, even though any local will tell you it's more like one hundred.'

They rode through the forest, dropping down to single file when the track became narrow, and eventually Penny stopped talking and they walked in silence. It was nice just listening to the chatter of birds above and the occasional neigh of a horse from behind, and Poppy leaned down to give Crystal a quick cuddle. Eventing was amazing, and she loved the excitement of racing around the cross-country and showjumping courses, but being in the saddle and going for a long trail ride in the country was just as fun.

Poppy sat back up and was about to ask Penny whether they would go back the same way they'd come, when a movement up ahead caught her eye. Her heart started to pound. She tugged lightly on her reins, speechless as she stared ahead.

'Poppy?' Penny asked.

'Hey!' Milly complained, as Joe bumped into them.

'They're there,' Poppy croaked. 'The brumbies are ahead.'

Penny held up her hand high and the chatter

behind her, the rise and fall of hooves, stopped suddenly.

Poppy gulped as she watched the brumbies move properly into view and then stop, heads raised, no doubt smelling that they had company.

Poppy squinted in the rising sun, leaning forward slightly to get a better look. Crystal edged forward and suddenly she was looking right at a beautiful chestnut, his head held defiantly high as he studied them. There was some distance between them, but it didn't take away from how special the moment was.

'That's the lead stallion. You see how he's a little apart from the others?' Penny said in a low voice.

Poppy nodded. She had read so much about the mobs and how they worked, and she was bursting with excitement to see the stallion staring them down like that, ready to protect his mares and young against any threat.

The mob soon moved off, and Poppy counted nine of them. Just a small group, but still so special. Her heart was leaping when she saw a young foal skip alongside his mother, and she could hardly breathe as she watched the stallion survey them one last time before following his mob. In total silence they melted away into the forest.

'That was incredible,' Poppy sighed.

'We were very lucky to see a mob so early in the day,' Penny said. She urged her horse forward and Crystal fell into step beside her. Penny continued sharing information about the forest with them, but Poppy hardly heard a word. Her head was filled with the chestnut stallion and his beautiful mares. There had been bays and dark browns amongst the group, and she turned to look back at Storm. Aunt Sophie raised her hand in a wave and Poppy smiled. She studied the white blaze on Storm's face and his strong jaw, and wondered if they could have been related to him. Could that stallion have been his sire? Could any of those mares have been his dam?

She wished she'd been riding him so she could have felt the change in his body when they'd seen the mob of brumbies. Had he tensed up, his muscles bunched and ready to gallop off after them? Had he held himself rigid, like he knew where he was and what he was seeing?

A ripple of excitement made her shiver and she stared ahead, scanning the forest for any more signs of movement. Others were desperate to see kangaroos and koalas, but all she wanted was to spot brumbies, and the week had got off to a pretty good start so far.

'Hey, look at that!' Katie whispered, swatting at Poppy's hand and making her drop the cookie she was eating.

Poppy stared silently at the bushy-tailed fox that trotted between trees in the distance. Dusk was sweeping across the sky and Poppy's eyelids were starting to feel heavy as they sat together away from the yards, but seeing the fox made her wake up fast. She loved all animals, and seeing them in the wild was incredible. Their ride had been amazing and she'd seen so many birds and other animals, but to see a fox up close was even more special.

'I thought they were terrified of humans?' Milly asked as it disappeared.

Poppy picked up her cookie and dusted it off. 'Me too. But he's not exactly coming close, and he's probably hungry.'

'What are you three whispering about?' Uncle

Mark appeared behind them, holding out a plate of fruit.

'There was a fox, just over there,' Katie said, pointing. 'He was so beautiful.'

Poppy imagined what it would be like to run her fingers through the thick red fur of a fox. When she was younger she'd always dreamed of having a fox as a pet.

'Have you ever rescued one?' Milly asked. 'Or, like, done your vet thing on one of them?'

Uncle Mark laughed. 'Yes, Milly, I've *done my vet thing* with a fox before. You make it sound so unofficial.'

Poppy stifled a giggle, not wanting to make Milly feel silly.

'Well, you know, I meant, like . . .'

Uncle Mark shook his head and ruffled Milly's hair teasingly. 'I knew what you meant. And actually, working on a fox isn't my favourite kind of job.'

'Why?' Poppy asked, reaching for some mango and straining to catch another glimpse of the fox.

'Well, they stink to start with,' Mark said, wrinkling his nose. 'There's this smell about them – it's hard to describe, but it's very strong. And they're extremely timid. I had a client who rescued some young pups once and secretly kept them, and I was always happy to help him when he needed it. But there are more fox haters than lovers around.'

Poppy groaned. 'It's like the brumby all over again! Why can't people just leave animals to be animals? Why do they want to kill them?'

Her uncle's arm looped around her and she leaned into him, her head resting on his shoulder. 'I know how frustrating it can all be, Poppy. Trust me, I do.'

'Sometimes I feel like we're the only ones in the world who even care,' she muttered, sighing.

'Look,' Katie said. 'Look!' she hissed.

Poppy blinked and stared at the spot where the fox had been. She could see something that looked like small brown smudges in the dying light. Surely they weren't . . . *Pups*. She looked back at Uncle Mark.

'Sometimes the universe gives you something to smile about,' he said, placing a hand on her shoulder for a moment before leaving them.

'I can't believe it,' Milly whispered, leaning in to her as the little animals wriggled and played. 'I've never seen fox pups before. Aren't they gorgeous?'

Poppy nodded and traded smiles with her friends as they watched the pups leaping and wrestling while their mother tried to usher them away. Something about seeing the mother fox made her think about her own mum.

Even though she was having fun, she still missed her, and it reminded Poppy of something Katie had said, about how her mum might be lonely without her around. Maybe it was kind of nice for her mum to have someone to hang out with. Poppy just wished it was a friend and not a *boy*friend.

'I hope we see more brumbies tomorrow,' Katie said.

'Me too,' Poppy agreed, yawning. Her body was aching from hours in the saddle, and probably from the rough sleep she'd had the night before. The ground wasn't exactly comfortable, even on her little roll-up mattress.

They sat silently, munching on fruit and staring into the gathering darkness for any other signs of wildlife.

Just as Poppy was about to suggest they head to bed, she heard a nicker and then a loud whinny.

She glanced over to where the horses were, but it was too dark now to see them.

'What is it?' Katie asked as Poppy leapt up.

'I was just . . . I don't know . . . I thought that sounded like Storm.'

Milly reached out and Poppy helped haul her to her feet.

'Want to take a look?' Milly asked.

There was another loud whinny. This time Poppy was certain it was Storm's call. 'We need to check on them before bed anyway, right?'

Katie leapt up and they made their way over to their tent to get torches. There was plenty of light around the camp – the muster yards were full of lamps and there were lights strung up across the fences, casting spooky shadows.

'We're just going to check on the horses,' Poppy called over to her aunt and uncle.

They were busy chatting to another couple and she received a wave of her hand and smile in response from Aunt Sophie.

The horses were quiet; the only noise the soft rustling and chewing of hay as Poppy led the way down to where their ponies were being kept. She shone the torch ahead and looked for Storm's familiar face.

'Eeek, sorry, Joe!' she apologised, swiftly dipping the torch when she shone it right in his eyes. She pointed it up a little and saw Crystal, then Storm.

'He looks fine,' Milly said. 'What were you worried about?'

Poppy bit her bottom lip and sucked it in, watching him. Storm was standing with his head held high, ears pricked.

'Something's not right,' she said, passing Milly the torch and watching as he pawed the ground. 'Can you keep it on me, so I can see?'

'He's very alert,' Katie said. 'Do you think he can hear something we can't?'

'Wouldn't the others all hear it if he could?' Milly replied.

Poppy walked over to Storm and stroked his cheek. Then she moved closer and slid her arm under and around his neck, leaning into him, breathing in his sweet horsey scent and staring into the dark with him.

'I think he knows where he is,' she told her friends. 'I think that maybe he's remembering, or that this place seems weirdly familiar to him or something. Maybe he can hear a horse he recognises?'

Her friends didn't say anything and Poppy's cheeks warmed as she realised how stupid she probably sounded. 'That was silly, I just . . .'

'It's not silly,' Katie said right behind her, making her jump.

'You don't think so?'

'Horses have amazing senses, so he probably knows where he is. Maybe he's calling out to his old mob?' Milly's voice was low, but Poppy could tell she was excited. 'Maybe there's a mob of brumbies right there somewhere, watching us now, but we can't see them?'

Poppy pressed her cheek to Storm's and imagined the stallion or maybe a lead mare standing in the dark, completely hidden by the blanket of nightfall. Maybe one of them did recognise Storm's call? They knew very little about how long he'd been out of the forest or what had truly happened to him, so there was a good chance the mob he'd grown up with was still here, since the brumbies weren't allowed to be mustered out.

'What do you see?' Poppy asked him. 'Is your family out there?'

Silence stretched between them, and Storm shifted his weight, nickered and then dipped his head to his hay. Poppy noticed that his ears were still flicked forward though, his attention not solely on his food.

'I think we should investigate,' Milly said from the other side of the fence.

Poppy gave Storm a final pat then she and Katie ducked low beneath the temporary fencing to join Milly.

'You mean go see if there's a mob of brumbies secretly watching us in the dark?' Katie asked. 'No thanks.'

Poppy looked around, suddenly noticing just how dark it was. The low hum of noise and the flicker of lights from the muster yards wasn't far away, but she suddenly hated the thought that something could be watching them. It spooked her big time. She shivered and wrapped her arms tight around herself.

'Why are you guys suddenly so spooked?' Milly asked.

'I'm not scared,' Katie said defiantly. 'But there's being adventurous and then there's being stupid.'

Milly huffed and Poppy giggled, grabbing hold of her and yanking her in for a hug. 'Hey, don't go getting all grumpy on us! I just don't want to walk off into the dark and get in trouble so that I miss out on more riding.'

'Tomorrow then?' Milly asked. 'Why don't we explore a bit? We're not riding until the afternoon, so we could go take a look around?'

'But the rules are that we can only go on scheduled group rides,' Katie said. 'Otherwise the organisers get in big trouble and they might not be allowed to do another event here.'

Milly looked between Poppy and Katie, her grin wicked in the torchlight. 'Who said anything about exploring on horseback?'

Poppy's eyes widened as she digested Milly's words. 'I suppose you're right. They did only tell us not to *ride* on our own.'

'Poppy, are you seriously taking her side?' Katie questioned, her mouth hanging open. 'We could get in big trouble for this!'

Poppy glanced back into the darkness and

wondered again about Storm's relatives. She was desperate to see more of the Barmah brumbies, and even though she didn't want to get in trouble, she *really* wanted to explore.

'Just for an hour,' she said. 'If we're not long, then no one will even realise we're missing.'

'So you're in?' Milly whispered.

'Katie?' Poppy asked.

They were all silent for a beat until Katie banged her shoulder in Poppy's and groaned. 'Okay, yes, I'm in.'

'Me too,' Poppy whispered.

Milly let out a whoop and Poppy slammed her hand over her friend's mouth to hush her. Her skin broke out in goosebumps and excitement bubbled through her. Tomorrow they were going to search for brumbies.

CHAPTER EIGHT

Forest Fun

'Are you absolutely certain we should do this?' Poppy asked, chewing on her bottom lip as they fed the horses hay and lugged water over to them.

Milly stuck her hands on her hips and gave her a long, cool stare. Even if she hadn't actually said anything, Poppy totally got the message. Loud and clear.

'You're not backing out now. Come on! Where's your sense of adventure?'

Poppy hesitated before saying what was on her mind. 'Look, I don't want to get into a crazy amount of trouble. I think we should just tell someone that we're going for a walk.'

Milly groaned loudly, but Katie was quick to agree with Poppy. 'Let's tell Mrs D we're going for a walk down to the river. She'll be fine with that, and no one said we're not allowed to go for walks, did they?'

To Poppy's surprise, Milly shrugged and blew out a big breath. 'I know when I'm outnumbered. But you're probably right – we shouldn't walk off without telling someone. I say we tell Mr D though. He's not as strict.'

'One other thing,' Katie said.

'What?' Poppy asked, setting down the bucket she was carrying and used the hair tie around her wrist to secure her hair back. She was sick of it falling around her face, and the back of her neck was getting hot and sticky.

'I think we should use markers if we leave the main track. You know, so we don't end up lost in the forest,' Katie said. 'Maybe we could use a red marker on the tree trunks that we turn past, or we could sprinkle something?'

Poppy wasn't so sure. 'I don't think we can mark the forest. We'd have to do something that wasn't permanent.'

Poppy picked up her bucket and went to do one final scoop of water for the troughs. What could they use?

'Wasn't there a ball of string in the tack box?' Katie suddenly said. 'I remember seeing it in there and wondering what it was for.'

Poppy nodded. 'Genius! I'll get it. We can tie bits of string around branches to find our way back.'

'Now you've got the markers figured out, do you want to talk to Mr D or shall I?' Milly asked. 'I think we should ask if we can go straight after lunch. The adults will be so busy sitting around drinking coffee and chatting, they won't notice if we're gone for a bit. And we'll just make sure we're back for the afternoon ride.' She flicked water at Poppy.

Poppy dodged the spray but water sloshed out of her bucket, wetting her leg and trickling into her boot.

'Milly!' she yelled grumpily, trying to run after her friend without losing any more of her water.

But Milly was long gone, laughing and tipping water into the makeshift troughs before sprinting back in towards their tent. Poppy guessed that meant asking Uncle Mark was definitely up to her.

'Want me to help you get her?' Katie asked, falling into step beside Poppy as they walked back.

'One day I'm gonna get her back so bad,' Poppy muttered. 'Like dead-frog-in-her-sock or something-gross-in-her-bed kind of bad.'

Katie giggled and linked her arm through Poppy's. 'Yeah, but if we did that to her, imagine what she'd think up next?'

Poppy knew they weren't doing anything wrong. Yet. But as they walked slowly away from the campsite for a stroll to the river, she couldn't help glancing over her shoulder to see if anyone was watching them.

'You look guilty,' Milly said. 'Just keep walking and stop looking back.'

'Do you really think we'll be able to find them on foot?' Poppy asked, trying to take Milly's advice.

'Maybe,' Katie said. 'Even if there are only a hundred of them in the forest, we've already seen a handful. There must be small mobs everywhere.'

She was probably right. 'Want to go to the river and walk a bit along there?' Poppy asked. 'We probably should have got a map or something.' They may as well have been blindfolded, she realised, as they had no idea where to go or what they might find on the way!

'A map like this?' Katie asked, whipping something out from her back pocket, waggling her eyebrows and making them laugh. 'Ta da! I got it from one of the camp guides. They had a stack of them with all the first-aid kits and things.'

Poppy snatched it from her and took a look, pleased that they at least had something to go by. She adjusted the strap of her backpack and looked ahead to the river. It really was beautiful. She'd read that it was over one hundred kilometres long. She remembered the sign she passed every time she drove from Melbourne to Geelong to visit Starlight Stables; that was only eighty kilometres and it took almost an hour to drive that far. Imagine walking the entire length of the river!

'Is that an emu?' Katie asked, pointing at something rustling in the bush.

Poppy froze for a moment, hoping that Katie wasn't right.

'They're so freaky with their glassy eyes and

long necks!' she exclaimed when it stood up and wandered off.

She saw another one and shuddered, hoping it didn't chase them. She loved almost all animals, but big birds like that weren't her favourites. They were scary and the last thing she wanted was one of them chasing after them!

'Let's go over this way,' she said. 'I don't think we should go near them.'

'Don't you think it's crazy how many wild animals we have in Australia?' Milly asked, following Poppy as she detoured them away from the emus. 'Like, we have to be careful about snakes and stuff, even crocodiles in the rivers up north, but my mum told me that New Zealand doesn't have any scary native animals.'

Poppy laughed. 'That kiwi bird has a pretty long beak. I wouldn't want to come across him at night!'

Katie giggled and ran at her, hands tucked up under her armpits like wings as she pretended to peck. 'Watch out! Big scary kiwi bird coming!' she squawked.

Poppy swatted her away, laughing so hard her cheeks hurt.

'If you carry on like that, all the brumbies in the forest will gallop in the other direction,' Milly moaned, taking the lead. 'Come on, and stay quiet.'

Poppy made a face. For once they'd traded places. It was usually them barking at Milly to keep her mouth shut.

'Let's go this way,' Milly said, taking them away from the river. 'I have a feeling about it.'

Poppy wasn't so sure, but then she wasn't actually sure about anywhere they were heading. All she knew was that her heart was beating overtime at the thought of getting close to another mob of brumbies.

She tied a piece of string around a branch, fingers fumbling as she worked the knot. Before they'd left she'd used a knife to cut it into pieces.

'I wonder what the brumbies' hooves are like with no one trimming them,' Poppy said as she caught up to her friends. 'I mean, we do so much for our horses, but these guys just do their own thing.'

They walked slowly, trying to be quiet, but every footfall made a tiny noise that Poppy knew horses would easily hear and be alerted to.

'I've read that they cover so much ground they

naturally wear down and break off,' Milly said. 'But did you see those pictures in the news last summer? The ones of the dead brumbies?'

Poppy shuddered. She remembered seeing the images of the horses with swollen bellies, dead after a bad drought. She pushed the thoughts away. 'It's always water they struggle to find during summer. Penny said the other day that it's the biggest killer, but I guess it's the same for all animals. Although the ones here would always have water because of the river.'

They chatted and walked, keeping their voices low. The sun was warm on Poppy's back and even though they hadn't seen anything yet, she felt happy.

'How many strings have you tied?' Katie asked suddenly.

Poppy stopped walking. She'd been so busy talking and looking around that she'd forgotten all about the string!

Katie looked at her. 'Poppy?'

'Um, well . . .' She spun around, wondering how far they'd walked.

'You forgot, didn't you?' Katie asked as Poppy

got out her drink bottle and took a sip.

Poppy gulped. 'Um, I just . . .' She could see a clearing up ahead and prayed they'd be able to get their bearings there. She pushed her fingers through the straps of her backpack. 'I got distracted looking around. I'm sorry.'

'We'll be fine,' Milly said, holding up the map in her hand. 'It can't be that hard to find our way back out. We just need to find the river again and that will lead us back to camp.'

Poppy hoped she was right. She fastened the top on her bottle and put it in her pack, then took out a bag of trail mix and offered some to her friends. Milly put her hand in straightaway and took a handful, but Katie shook her head, looking worried.

'Look, we haven't been walking that long, and it won't be hard to retrace our steps,' Poppy said. But when she glanced at her watch, she could see they'd been going for over an hour. And she couldn't even remember the last time she tied a string.

She looked up, scanning the trees for animals. She knew there would be koalas somewhere in the gum trees, no doubt snoozing during the day while it was so warm. And there might be kangaroos nearby too.

The idea that they weren't alone in the bush made her feel better, even if those animals knew the forest like the back of their little paws and she didn't have a clue where they were.

'Come on, let's walk for a little longer and see if we see anything,' Milly said, taking the lead again. 'We have a map and we're smart. We can still get back in time for our late afternoon ride. You guys seriously need to chill out. We'll be fine!'

They continued on, and Poppy distracted herself with thoughts about the brumbies they'd seen the day before, and then Storm, thinking how magnificent he would have looked standing amongst the mob, his dark ears pricked at the sight of humans.

It wasn't until another half an hour had passed and they were still walking through unfamiliar bush that Poppy started to get worried. She sneaked a peek at Katie, who was biting her bottom lip and peering around as she walked.

Poppy opened her mouth to say something.

'You girls lost?'

'ARGH!'

The sudden, deep voice made Poppy scream. She clamped a hand over her mouth and spun sideways and saw a tall man leaning against a tree, a drink bottle raised to his mouth.

CHAPTER NINE

We're in Trouble Now

'Um . . .' Poppy stuttered, grabbing hold of Katie's arm and wondering if they should run back the way they'd come. Why had they ever decided to explore on their own? She'd thought about the animals they might encounter, but not other humans!

'We're fine,' Katie said bravely, her voice sounding strong and sure.

Poppy knew if she tried to speak, she'd be all croaky and scared sounding, but she cleared her throat anyway and stood up tall, her shoulders straight, trying to look brave.

The man hadn't moved, but he had finished sipping his drink and his smile seemed friendly.

'I don't often come across kids on their own out here, unless they're trying to run away.'

His voice was warm and easy, and Poppy wondered at what he'd said. Was he in the forest a lot?

Milly's planted her hands on her hips. 'Who are you, and why are you here?' she asked.

Poppy would have laughed if she weren't so scared. Trust Milly.

'I should be the one asking who you are, but fair enough,' the man said, stepping out into the clearing. His skin was dark and weathered, like he spent a lot of time outdoors, and she guessed he was close in age to Uncle Mark. He moved in an unhurried way and looked completely at home in the forest.

'I'm Jack,' he said, holding out his hand. 'I'm one of the park rangers here, but I'm not working today.' He put his other hand in his pocket and pulled out an identification card that he passed to Poppy. It had his name, photo and the words 'Park Ranger' across the top.

Relief flooded through Poppy. She stuck out her hand and shook Jack's. 'I'm Poppy,' she said, 'and this is Milly and Katie.'

He nodded. 'Nice to meet you all.' He crossed his arms over his chest and considered them. 'You don't strike me as runaways, but I still have the feeling you're lost. Am I right?'

'Not exactly,' Milly said quickly.

'We are *completely* lost,' Katie said. 'We had this idea of going in search of brumbies and tying string to the trees so we could follow our path back and then . . .'

'Katie!' Milly hissed, holding up her map. 'We're not lost!'

Jack raised an eyebrow and Poppy smiled. '*Technically* we're not sure if we're lost just yet, because we haven't tried to find our way back.'

His laugh was deep. 'You're in search of brumbies though? Is that one thing you can all agree on?'

Poppy nodded and the other two mumbled their agreement.

'Just so happens I'm in search of brumbies myself,' he said. '*Technically* I'm not supposed to interfere with them, but it's my day off and I want to keep an eye on a young colt who's been injured.

There're a couple of youngsters who aren't looking that great. I should take you girls straight back to the muster yards. But since you're here you may as well come along with me. The horses are nearby.'

Poppy looked at the others excitedly and they hurried after him as he moved quietly off.

'How did you know we need to go back to the muster yards?' Milly blurted at his back.

He laughed. 'Because you're wearing riding boots and jodhpurs, and this is one of the only times of year horse riders are allowed in here.'

Milly's cheeks flamed red. Poppy wondered if it would be rude to ask Jack more questions. She was dying to know how long he'd been a park ranger and what his work involved. Did he get up close with the brumbies and other animals? What an awesome job!

'What are you going to do if you find them?' Katie asked.

'There's a chance we might be mustering some of them out of here. It's not something we've done before, but the local brumby association are keen to help, and I'm this close,' he said, holding two fingers an inch apart, 'to making it happen.'

They walked with Jack and Poppy realised she was no longer afraid of him. He seemed nice and knowledgeable, and she trusted him.

'What made you want to be a ranger?' she asked.

He put up his hand and they all stopped. Poppy wondered what he'd heard or seen.

'My ancestors had a connection with this land,' he said, his voice low and his gaze fixed on something in the distance. Poppy tried and failed to see what he was looking at. 'My ancestory is Yorta Yorta on my father's side. They are the Traditional Owners, and when my father passed away and this job came up a week later, I took it as a sign I was supposed to be here. I love working out in the open and this place is even more special with my connection to it.'

Milly took a step forward and her shoulder brushed Poppy's.

'I don't want this to sound insensitive, but what do our Aboriginal elders think about brumbies? Do they think they're pests or . . .' Her voice trailed off. 'I hope that didn't come out all wrong, it sounded better in my head.'

'She's asking because we're hearing so much

about people wanting to cull the brumbies here,' Poppy said quickly.

'And you seem to care for them and your people . . .'

'They're not native to this land, but they're connected to it,' Jack said, not looking at all offended by Milly's question. 'And don't ever feel you can't ask questions, okay? That's not being insensitive. The more questions we all ask, the better we understand one another.'

Poppy threw Milly a smile.

'I like that, saying they're connected to the land,' Katie said shyly.

'You know, some of my ancestors fought in Turkey during World War One,' Jack told them. 'Central desert brumbies were used there, and many Aboriginal communities feel very connected to our national horse because of that, and because of how long they've been roaming on our land. They're special the way they've adapted to survive here, and we respect that.'

Poppy opened her mouth to say something, but Jack raised a hand and she quickly shut it.

'Shh,' he whispered.

Poppy glanced at Milly and then Katie, but she could see that they didn't know what they were supposed to be looking at either. She peered back at the clump of trees about fifty metres away.

And then he appeared.

The stallion was almost black, the identical colour to Storm, only he didn't have any white markings, and the tips of his mane and tail were bleached to a dark gold. He was a different stallion to the one they'd seen the day before, but just as magnificent. He held himself so tall, his muscled shoulder strong as he stamped his hoof once and then looked around, surveying the land and bush. He snorted, and she wondered if he'd sensed them.

'I can't believe it,' Milly whispered. 'We've actually found a mob!'

Poppy was about to point out that actually Jack had found the mob, when he held up his hand again.

'The mares are behind him. They'll move out in a moment,' he told them.

Poppy stayed deathly still, her breathing shallow as she watched. The stallion dipped his head to graze, but she could see that he was still alert. He knew they were there and he wasn't about to turn away from them, but he was showing them that he wasn't afraid.

'I thought the mares were in charge?' Katie whispered. 'But both times we've seen a mob, it's been the stallion at the front.'

'He's the protector of his mob,' Jack said. 'He will fight off any danger and look after his family. But the lead mare is in charge of the mob. The mares are very important to the group, and their foals are given the same respect as their mothers. Alone they are nothing, but beside their mother they are protected.'

They all watched in silence as the mob moved, grazing for some time and then walking a few steps before grazing again. Poppy was surprised how quiet they were. The entire mob was so peaceful, without any kicking or biting. She'd expected the stallion or colts to be aggressive. Maybe it was because they weren't confined to a paddock and they could move freely with space between each other when they needed it.

'They're so beautiful,' Poppy said to no one in particular. Tears filled her eyes as a mare came out into the clearing. A foal burst from the bush behind her, all long gangly legs and knocking knees. She watched as he drank from his mother's teat, and the mare gazed down at him. It was incredible. They might end up in a world of trouble for being gone so long, thought Poppy, but seeing this had been worth any punishment.

'I'll never forget this,' Katie whispered.

'Me neither,' Poppy said, wiping at her eyes with the back of her hands.

Milly was silent, and Poppy glanced at her, surprised to see tears streaming down her cheeks.

'Thanks for making us run away,' Poppy whispered to her. 'This is better than anything I've ever seen before in my life.'

She had no idea how long they stood there, watching the horses. There were fifteen horses all up, including foals. Poppy couldn't stop smiling. She knew that she'd never forget what it was like to see a group of horses in the wild.

'Where is the injured one you were talking about?' Katie asked.

Jack looked worried and Poppy could tell he genuinely cared about the brumbies. He pointed further down to the right, past the mob.

'Down there. They're young colts and they're staying away from the mob. I don't know what's happened to them. Maybe someone has hurt them, or maybe it's nature taking its course, but either way I'd like to muster them out and see if we can help them. Especially the obviously injured one, because I think it could be the start of something great if we manage to save them, then maybe train and re-home them.'

Poppy followed his pointing finger, and her eyes finally locked on the pair of colts. They were in a denser part of the trees, whereas the rest of the horses had been in a clearing. Was it unusual for them to be so far from the mob?

She watched as they moved, making it easier for her to see, and even from the distance she noticed that they looked rangy – slightly underweight and with shaggy manes and chewed-off tails.

'Why aren't the rest of the mob looking after them?' she asked. 'I thought they all took care not to leave one another behind?'

'I think they could be bachelors,' Jack said. 'The two of them have moved away from the mob, and they should be off on their own. But something's happened to them, and because they're not a threat, the stallion is tolerating them being nearby. I just can't get close enough to see what's wrong, but when they move some more, you'll see one is lame. He's having trouble with one hoof, I think.'

They stood for a long time, watching and waiting, until Jack turned to them and frowned. 'I'd better get you girls back,' he said. 'Come on.'

Jack took a couple more photos on his phone then moved to lead them away. Poppy looked over her shoulder one last time to drink in the sight of the stallion. She hoped that the Barmah brumbies were allowed to stay in their forest home forever.

'Hey, have you seen the time?' Katie asked.

Poppy glanced down at her watch and grimaced. They were definitely going to be in serious trouble. She'd told Uncle Mark they were heading off for a short stroll to the river, but they'd been gone the entire afternoon! How long had they been watching the horses for?

'We're dead,' she hissed.

'Who's dead?' Milly asked.

'US!' Poppy replied, walking faster to keep up with Jack. He moved quickly and confidently through the forest, even though every tree looked the same to Poppy.

They walked and walked, and her legs started to ache. It hadn't seemed so long on their way in, but she felt like they'd been walking forever now.

'You know, I think Mrs D will understand when we tell her what we were doing,' Milly said, sounding so sure of herself. 'Trust me.'

Poppy doubted it. They kept up their fast walk, and Poppy kept hoping that somehow no one had noticed their absence.

Until she heard a call that made her heart stop beating.

'Poppy! Milly! Katie!'

The frantic yell sent a wave of guilt rushing through her. It was Aunt Sophie. And from the sounds of her hoarse voice, she'd been at it a while.

CHAPTER TEN

Guilty

'We're here!' Poppy yelled out. 'We're here!'

'Poppy?' Aunt Sophie called back.

Poppy pushed past her friends and searched frantically for her aunt. She could still hear her calling and she sounded so near but . . .

Jack touched Poppy's arm and pointed to the right. 'Over there.'

Poppy saw her aunt's figure through the trees. 'Aunt Sophie!' she called out, running straight at her aunt and throwing her arms around Sophie. 'I'm so sorry. We should never have gone so far without telling you.'

Sophie held her tight and Poppy could hear her

heart beating loud against her ear.

'Where have you girls been? Mark and I have been looking everywhere for you!'

Poppy stepped back. She knew she had guilt written all over her face, and she couldn't exactly lie and pretend like they'd just got lost.

'Who is this?' Aunt Sophie suddenly said, taking Poppy's hand.

'Oh, that's Jack,' she explained as the others appeared. 'He's a park ranger and he kind of helped us get back.'

'Hi,' Jack said, holding up a hand. 'I take it these girls belong to you.'

Aunt Sophie sighed. 'Unfortunately, yes,' she said, giving them a stern look. 'Honestly, girls, sometimes I wonder why I offer to look after you so often.'

Milly looked guilty and Katie was staring at her feet. Poppy realised how awful it must have been for Sophie, thinking that they were lost out there in the forest with night approaching.

'Seems I found them on a brumby hunt,' Jack said with a deep chuckle. 'With all the crashing and banging through the forest though, I'm not sure how they thought they'd find any wild animals.'

Aunt Sophie rolled her eyes. 'Well, you'd better come back for a drink and something to eat, Jack. I'm sorry you had to bring them all this way.'

'It's not a problem. Besides, I was going to drop past to speak to Penny about a brumby problem she's been helping me with.'

Aunt Sophie nodded and Jack fell into step beside her. She called out to Mark and Poppy held her breath, hoping they weren't in too much trouble. Maybe Jack being there had been a good distraction. Maybe they weren't going to be punished after all. The camp emerged through the trees and Poppy quickened her step.

'Girls,' Aunt Sophie said. She had stopped walking and was staring at them. The girls stopped as one. 'Don't think this means you're not in trouble,' Aunt Sophie said firmly. 'Once I figure out your punishment, I'll let you know.'

Poppy gulped and she heard Milly's low moan.

'It won't be too bad, will it?' Katie whispered.

Poppy sighed. 'I hope not. But we'd better make ourselves useful and help out with the horses anyway.'

She figured that anything they did to get back in Aunt Sophie's good books was worth it.

'Go find your uncle,' Sophie called. 'And if you get lost looking for him, you'll have to find your own way back!'

'Great,' Milly muttered. 'She's definitely going to kill us – she's just waiting until Jack's gone.'

Katie shuddered beside her and Poppy stomped off to look for Uncle Mark.

'I just don't know what you were thinking,' Aunt Sophie scolded in a low voice. 'If the organisers knew how badly you'd behaved today, they'd probably tell us to go home.'

Poppy's eyes widened. *Home?!*

'We didn't mean to be gone for so long.' Her words sounded pathetic and she knew it.

'We just wanted to see some brumbies up close and we thought it would be a little adventure,' Milly said. 'It was my idea. I should get the blame.'

'No,' Poppy argued. 'We all went and we all agreed on the plan. It's not just Milly's fault.'

She elbowed Katie in the side.

'Ow!' Katie muttered.

Poppy stared at her.

'Um, yeah, it's not just Milly's fault,' mumbled Katie. But her glare told Poppy that she definitely thought Milly should be taking *all* the blame.

'Girls, this isn't the first time you've done something like this, and I need to know that I can trust you,' Sophie continued. 'Quite frankly, I don't care whose fault it is. I just want you to stop disappearing on me. Enough's enough.'

Poppy didn't have to pretend to look guilty. Aunt Sophie had done so much for her, for all of them.

'I'm sorry,' Poppy said. 'I really mean it, too. We shouldn't have wandered off so far and for so long.'

'You could have ended up lost out there for the night, and then we'd have had to get volunteers to help search for you.' Aunt Sophie shook her head. 'It's time to start acting your age, girls. Twelve is old enough to be sensible, and I should be able to trust you.'

'You can trust us,' Katie said. 'It won't happen again.'

'The thing is I do trust you, but I'm starting to doubt my own judgement,' Sophie said, opening the esky and passing them all bottles of water. 'But this is the last time, girls. Next time you tell me what you're planning. Heavens, I would have loved to come searching for brumbies with you! And we could have let some others know where we were going, and none of this would have happened. You're just lucky that Jack found you.'

They sat in silence for a moment, drinking their water. But Poppy couldn't sit on her question for long.

'What's going to happen to the injured brumbies?' she said, the words bursting from her.

'It looks like this will be the first time in years that some brumbies will be mustered from the forest,' Aunt Sophie told them. 'Penny is hopeful that if this goes well, they'll be able to establish a precedent for mustering a small number of brumbies out each year or two, for re-homing, rather than for slaughter. There's been a lot of talk of these brumbies being culled, and in other states the poor things are either shot from helicopters or mustered in and then killed. It might be a way to manage numbers, which is similar to what they do in New Zealand with their wild Kaimanawas.'

Poppy's heart leapt. That was great news!

'Are we going to be allowed to ride again?' she asked. 'I mean . . .'

'Yes, Poppy, you're allowed to go on the trail ride in the morning. In fact,' Aunt Sophie said as she screwed the top back on her water bottle, 'if you hadn't disappeared, you would have been off riding this afternoon, too. I hear the brumby spotting on the ride today was excellent.'

Poppy balled her fists. Why did they keep doing stupid stuff? Although . . . they had seen that amazing mob and it had kind of been worth it.

'First thing tomorrow we'll ride out with the group. We didn't come all this way to ground you, and I want you to have fun and enjoy being here.'

'But?' Milly asked. 'There's *always* a but.'

'But I haven't decided yet whether I'll let you be part of the muster of the injured brumbies. Penny requested you three by name. Seems she's been impressed with your riding and your interest in the brumbies. She likes fostering interest in the new generation of brumby lovers.'

Poppy dug her nails into her palms, not wanting to say the wrong thing.

'Please, Mrs D,' Milly begged. 'I'll do anything!'

Poppy stared at her aunt. Surely she'd let them. 'Please, Aunt Soph,' she murmured, clearing her throat. 'I'm truly sorry for what we did, but helping to round up those young brumbies would be so incredible. I can't stop thinking about how that could have been Storm a few years ago. And how many more might end up at an auction, but this time no one will be there to save them.'

Sophie looked at Poppy, then gave the same long, considering look to her friends.

'Okay,' she finally said.

'Okay?' Poppy squealed.

'Okay. But *only* because this is a once in a lifetime opportunity.'

Poppy leaped to her feet and jumped up and down. Milly was right beside her, hand clamped over her mouth, and Katie's face said it all.

'Thank you,' Poppy said to her aunt, bending to give her a big hug.

'Just don't let me down again, girls. I mean it.'

Poppy nodded. 'Promise.'

'So when do we do this?' Katie asked, sounding breathless.

'On the final day when everyone has packed up and most of the horses and riders have gone,' Sophie replied. 'There'll be a small group remaining so it's as stress-free as possible for the brumbies, and we'll do our best to muster them in.'

Poppy thought she would burst with excitement. She was going to be part of a real brumby muster!

CHAPTER ELEVEN

Brumby Love

Poppy was exhausted. After four days at Barmah National Park, her bottom and legs were aching from so many hours in the saddle, and the rest of her was stiff from sleeping rough in the tent. She yawned and opened her eyes, stretching and listening to the murmur outside. The last couple of days had been amazing, and it had been so cool sleeping close to her horses and riding so much, but she was dying to go in search of the brumby mob again. Yesterday they'd seen them in the distance, but soon she might be able to see the colts up close and she couldn't wait.

Today is the last day!

She sat bolt upright and unzipped her sleeping

bag so she could wriggle out, not wanting to miss a second of their last hours at Barmah.

'Poppy?' Katie's voice was husky, like she'd just woken up too.

'Is anyone else up?' Milly asked with a loud yawn.

'I can hear some people talking out there, but I'm not sure who's up yet.'

Poppy unzipped the tent and poked her head out, taking a quick look around. The sun had only just started to rise so it was still pretty dark, but the pinkish sky was casting enough light around the muster yards for her to see. A pang of sadness echoed through her as she stared at the tents, listening to the whinny and shuffle of horses nearby. Tomorrow, everything would be gone, and it would be like no one had ever been here. She hoped that Aunt Sophie would bring them again next year, but after disappearing on their own to go brumby spotting, she wasn't so sure.

'Just a few people starting to get up,' Poppy said in a low voice to her friends. 'The first ride was heading out early, wasn't it?'

'I think so,' Katie replied. 'Let's get up and we

can help pack everything away.'

Poppy quickly agreed. She was happy to do anything that put her back in her aunt and uncle's good books. They got dressed and rolled up their sleeping-bags, pulled the tent down, then went off to feed the horses.

'Morning, Crystal!' she called out as she gave her hay. 'Morning, Stormy,' she said, giving him the same amount and a quick pat on the neck. She smiled as he lifted his head to nuzzle her. 'It's your last day here,' Poppy whispered to him. 'I hope you've called out your goodbyes.'

It had been so special being with him every day, even though she hadn't been riding him. If they came next year, would she have to choose between him and Crystal? As much as she wanted to ride Storm and have fun on him, she hated the thought of leaving Crystal behind. Maybe if they came again, she and Aunt Sophie could take turns on Storm and Crystal! That would be the perfect plan – if they were lucky enough to come back.

Poppy glanced back over at Storm, wondering how he felt, if he really knew where he was or if she was just imagining it. She still wasn't sure.

'Do you think he really knows where he is?' Milly asked, joining her and speaking her thoughts out loud.

Poppy sighed. 'Maybe. I don't know. It'd be cool if he knew we'd brought him back.'

'I had this dream about him, that he jumped out of the yards and joined his mob again and we had to gallop off and try to find him.'

Poppy smiled as the image of the three friends, bareback and galloping after Storm, entered her mind.

'You know what?'

'What?' Milly asked.

'If he did that, I'd just leave him,' Poppy said. She blinked away the familiar prickle of tears as she watched Storm eating, wondering if he was happy with her or not. She loved him, and he had a great life at Starlight Stables, but she often wondered if he wished he were still wild. 'I'd hate to steal him away from his family if he found them again.'

'Pops, if he still lived here, maybe he wouldn't be happy?' Katie said, joining them. 'He's always warm and safe at Starlight, and he has enough water and plenty to eat. Don't go feeling bad about it. Maybe there's a reason brumbies make such awesome horses to ride? They're probably happy when they find a human who loves them, so long as they're still surrounded by other horses.'

'Yeah, him being happy is the most important thing, and I think he probably loves being with you,' Milly said, slinging her arm around Poppy. 'He gets so much attention and lots of love!'

Poppy hoped they were right, but suddenly it was her mum she was thinking about, not Storm. She had hardly thought about her all week, but now that it was almost home time, it all rushed back into her head. As much as she hated the idea of her mum dating another man, her friends had been right. She *did* have so much – Starlight Stables, her friends and her horses – and she was so happy. Her mum deserved that, too, and even though Poppy didn't want to meet her mum's boyfriend yet, she was going to help tell Tom and also let her mum know that she wanted her to be happy. Her dad would be proud of her for saying it, and it was the right thing to do.

'So girls, are you ready to help me today?'

Poppy spun around at the same time her friends

did. Penny was standing there, her smile broad, already dressed in her jods and boots, a coffee mug in her hand. But it was the person beside her that made Poppy stare.

'Um, yes,' Poppy managed to say. 'We're ready.'

'This is Sienna,' Penny introduced the older girl beside her. 'She's one of the rider's who'll be staying behind to help today. She's very experienced with brumbies and I thought you might like to hear about some of her brumby work while we're riding out.'

Poppy looked at Milly and Katie, wide-eyed. This was amazing!

'That'd be so cool,' Milly said, the first of them to speak. Poppy watched as she stuck out her hand. 'I'm Milly and I know *everything* about you.'

Sienna laughed and shook it and then held her hand to Poppy. They all introduced themselves and Penny wandered off, leaving them standing with Sienna. It was amazing to think she was only six years older than them.

'So, I heard that one of you has a brumby,' Sienna said, her smile warm.

'That's Poppy,' Katie said, hooking her thumb in Poppy's direction.

'Can I see him?' Sienna asked.

Poppy sucked back a breath and then told herself to stop being so stupid. Sienna was just another girl. Sure, she was a crazy-amazing rider, but there was no reason to go all star-struck and silly.

'He's over here,' she said, clearing her throat. 'I'd love you to meet him.'

They walked and Sienna chatted to them about riding and their horses, until they reached the yards.

'That's him?' Sienna asked, pointing.

Poppy ducked under the fence and slipped an arm around Storm's neck. 'This is him. He actually came from this forest.'

Sienna held out her hand for him to sniff then stroked his neck, before walking around him and looking him over. 'He's beautiful. I love his white markings and how muscular he is. Do you ride him?'

'I have, but he's still a bit of a handful in the arena at home,' she admitted. 'I was the first to get on him bareback though.'

Sienna grinned.

'You know what? You should think about entering the next brumby challenge. I've heard they're going to open up a new category for youth trainers.'

Poppy's heart started to race. *Her?* She wasn't nearly good enough to enter anything like that! 'Um, I don't know. I probably don't know enough.'

'Bet you do,' Sienna said. 'And if you need some help, I'd be happy to train you. It'd be nice to have a young rider to work with, and you already have a brumby, so you'd be perfect.'

Poppy knew she had a stupid big grin on her face but she couldn't help it. 'Thanks, that'd be really cool,' she managed to mumble.

'See you girls soon. I'm just going to pack up and get ready.'

She ducked back under the fence and Poppy stared after her, trying to stop her jaw from hanging open.

'What was she saying to you?' Milly asked.

Poppy shook her head, not sure whether to tell her friends or not. 'We were talking about Storm,' she said. 'She liked the fact that I had a brumby.'

Milly and Katie started to talk excitedly about Sienna and going riding with her, but Poppy was only half-listening. All she could think about was one day being good enough to break in a wild brumby on her own, and working with Sienna to learn the ropes.

'Listen up, everyone,' Penny said. 'I want you to keep your eyes and ears on me at all times when we get near the brumbies.'

Jack had joined them, although he was on foot, and he spoke after her in a loud voice. 'The success of this muster will determine the future of what we do here with the brumbies, so I want everything to go as smoothly as possible,' he said. 'If we take a few head of horses out of here every year, and pledge to keep the numbers low, we might avoid a mass cull of horses in years to come, and it may keep everybody involved happy.'

Poppy listened, running one hand down Crystal's smooth neck. Her pony was relaxed, but her ears were still pricked and Poppy knew it would only take one nudge of her heels to get her pony to leap into action.

'So, here's how this will work,' Penny said.

Poppy looked around at the handful of riders

with them. Some were staying behind on foot to assist if they managed to bring the brumbies close, and there were ten mounted riders. Penny, Sienna, Poppy and her friends, as well as her aunt and uncle and two other riders from the brumby association. They were all listening to Penny speak.

'We're trying something different today, and it may or may not work,' she said. 'We have a limited window of opportunity, which means that we can't use passive trapping for these horses.'

'What's passive trapping?' Milly asked quietly.

'That's where they set up a trap with yards and try to lure the horses in slowly. The gate shuts behind the horses once they're in,' Poppy told her.

'We also don't believe that roping wild horses is humane, so that's out of the question,' Penny continued. 'Instead we're going to try to muster these young colts in, and see how we go. That means being fast and careful on horseback, and not rushing them in. The timing is perfect because at the last sighting this morning by Jack, they were isolated from other mobs.'

'There's every chance we won't manage to muster them in, but if we can do this, it would be an amazing opportunity to re-home them,' Jack said.

'Who's taking them if we catch them?' Katie asked.

'I am,' Sienna spoke up. 'I'll do anything I can to promote brumbies as fun, versatile horses, and we might get some good publicity from it, too.'

'So you'll train them and then sell them?' Poppy asked.

'Why, do you want to buy one from me?' Sienna asked with laugh.

'Don't go getting any ideas, Poppy,' said Aunt Sophie. Everyone laughed and Poppy shrugged sheepishly.

'This could be a long day, everyone,' said Penny, 'so let's go slow and stay alert.'

Poppy gathered up her reins. A quiver of excitement ran through her as they all started to head in the same direction they'd gone walking earlier in the week. Jack had said he'd seen the brumbies only a short distance away that morning, and Poppy hoped they'd be able to muster them in, but she knew it was unlikely. There were so many places for them to run and hide, and this was their home, so they had a huge advantage.

They rode under the shady canopy of trees through the forest. It felt like no time at all before Jack, who had been easily keeping up on foot, held up a hand. They all halted.

'No more talking. Not a word,' he said.

Poppy looked sideways at Milly and then Katie. Had he seen something? Was he just being cautious or was there actually a . . .

Jack motioned for them to spread out and he put his head down and quietly moved away in a big arc.

No way!

Poppy's heart felt like it was about to leap out of her chest. Her eyes were like saucers as she stared through the trees. The brumbies were right there. She saw the magnificent side profile of the two colts, heads held high in defiance, manes and forelocks scruffy and unkempt.

A high-pitched whinny and snort, followed by a series of smaller calls, echoed through the trees from behind Poppy, sending shivers through her entire body and making Crystal skitterish. She pulled back lightly on her reins, looking around, wondering whose horse was making such a fuss.

And then she saw who it was.

Storm.

Her beautiful brumby had called out, and the look on Aunt Sophie's face was a mixture of fear and excitement.

What would happen now?

CHAPTER TWELVE

Muster Mania

'Lead the way back, nice and slow,' Penny said in a soft voice.

Poppy's eyes darted from Sophie and back to Penny again. Penny waved at them all to go wide, and Poppy urged Crystal on, careful not to stare at the brumbies and moving well away from them so they could all come around and muster them in from behind. Some of the riders would take up the rear with Jack, and the others would fan out to the side. Except, it appeared, for Aunt Sophie.

The wild horses were slowly and steadily following Storm as he neighed and carried on as if he was trying to tell them something.

It was almost impossible to stay silent, but Poppy rode on, slipping her hand down to stroke Crystal's neck every now and then to calm her. She wondered why Storm's antics weren't scaring the colts, but for some reason he had their attention and they were eager to follow him.

Just as she was thinking how easy the whole thing had been, one of the colts, the one that didn't appear to be injured but was rangy with his ribs slightly protruding, darted out to the right. She sucked back a breath and kicked Crystal on, moving wide and around him, spurred into action.

She had to clamp her mouth shut to stop from speaking, she was so used to encouraging Crystal verbally.

Go!

She issued the command silently, screaming it inside her head.

Go!

Crystal was fast and the colt stopped when he saw them coming around in front of him. He veered back to his mate, but he was spooked now – prancing and rolling his eyes – and Poppy hoped she hadn't put too much pressure on him.

She looked back at Uncle Mark and received a quick thumbs up in reply, and she settled back into the saddle, happy that she must have done the right thing.

The whole point of what they were doing was to stop the horses from getting too stressed, but she guessed there was no way to stop them from being upset. They were wild animals, not used to any human interaction, and she felt a pang of guilt about what they were doing, knowing how terrified they would be if they did get them into the yards.

The colts attempted a couple of half-hearted dashes, but each time a rider appeared to herd them back. Storm continued to beckon and whinny and they followed willingly. Poppy wondered if it was because they weren't yet in a mob and didn't know how to look after themselves without being told what to do by a dominant stallion or mare.

Suddenly the yards came into sight and Poppy breathed a sigh of relief. The horse trucks and any evidence of humans were long gone, which meant the area shouldn't look too scary and unfamiliar to the horses, although she bet it smelt different to them.

She rolled her eyes at her thoughts. The timber railings alone were probably *way* scary to the brumbies.

Both young horses suddenly stopped, hooves digging into the ground and sending up a billow of dirt around them. Poppy held Crystal in check. She waited, watching, wondering what they were going to do. Sophie halted Storm, but he let out a high-pitched whinny and pawed at the ground. The colts hesitated and Poppy saw some of the other riders start to move forward from the corner of her eye. She nudged Crystal on, keeping her walk slow and her gaze steady.

This was the test. If they got them close enough to the yards, they'd have to be quick and nimble to actually get them in there without either brumby making a run for it and sidestepping.

She looked ahead to the yards and wondered how different it would have been to be mustering in cattle over a hundred years earlier to this same spot. She bet those riders were hot and sweaty after hours in the saddle searching for their herd, and they wouldn't have had the same camping comforts either.

Oh no!

Both brumbies darted in her direction. They were moving fast, bursting into a canter where they saw a gap, and she rode hard to block them, kicking Crystal and rising out of the saddle, reins thrust forward to give her horse her head.

They galloped straight and Crystal seemed to know exactly what to do. She skidded to a stop just in time to avoid a collision, doing a little rear as she put on her brakes, and the colts darted back the way they'd come from. Aunt Sophie rode Storm into the yards. He called out frantically to them again and again.

Poppy stayed alert, eyes never leaving the brumbies as she kept her spot. She tried not to groan when Milly and Katie almost lost them at one point and gasped when they narrowly avoided riding into one another, yanking their horses sideways just in time.

Please keep going. Please keep going. Poppy repeated the words over and over in her mind.

Where were the other riders who had stayed behind? She couldn't see them anywhere, but maybe the brumbies knew.

And then they suddenly appeared – three other riders on horseback emerging from the dense trees past the yards, ready to block that side. And then two more people on foot.

One of the colts neighed and did an impressive rear, but the one with the leg injury looked tired.

It was Penny who rode forward this time, slapping her thigh. 'Yah, yah!' she yelled out. 'Yah!'

Poppy's heart broke as she saw the frightened look on their faces, the whites of their eyes that were almost rolling in their heads, the panicked calls and the spinning around and around. She wished she could tell them what was happening, that there was nothing to be scared of. She wanted to cry, thinking of the poor brumbies that were run and roped, or even worse, killed by people in helicopters with a rifle in hand.

One of the brumbies moved forward, toward Storm and away from the group of horses and riders, and they all rode forward as if it had been perfectly planned. Poppy held Crystal steady as Penny and Jack flapped and yelled to get the other colt scared and moving.

Storm called one last time and the colts suddenly

turned and trotted through the gate.

A man leapt from nowhere and slammed the gate shut with a bang.

They'd done it! They'd actually managed to muster two wild brumbies into a yard to be re-homed!

Poppy glanced down and saw that her T-shirt was soaked in sweat, her hands shaking.

'That was awesome!' Milly said, riding up beside Poppy, her voice high with excitement.

'Better than awesome,' Katie replied. 'I can't believe it happened so easily.'

'It was Storm,' Poppy blurted. 'It was him, right? I mean, I wasn't imagining how they just started to follow him in, was I?'

Katie and Milly nodded their heads in agreement.

'Great work, girls! ' Penny praised, breathing hard as she rode past them.

'What happens now?' Katie asked.

'We organise a truck to transport these two,' said a voice from behind them, 'and I get them back to my place once Mark has taken a look over them from a distance. He did good today, your brumby.'

Poppy turned to see it was Sienna and smiled.

'Can we visit you and see what you do with them?' Milly blurted.

'Sure can,' Sienna said. 'Then maybe you can help me to convince Poppy that she should try her hand at breaking a brumby on her own one day soon?'

Poppy's cheeks ignited with heat and she looked down at her hands, clutching the reins tight.

'Isn't that right, Poppy?'

Milly and Katie both gave her long, hard stares, but Poppy refused to look back at them. It wasn't like it had been her idea, and she definitely didn't agree with Sienna that she should be working with brumbies. Not yet. Unless it was her Storm.

Sienna grinned and walked off, her back so straight in the saddle as she rode her brumby away. Poppy felt the familiar pang of guilt as she looked at the magnificent wild colts pressed hard against the timber fence. Would they be so scruffy-looking next time she saw them, or glossy and groomed like any other domestic horse? Would they buck and resist training or calmly take it all in their stride?

'I think you redeemed yourself today, girls,' Aunt

Sophie called out. She was sitting on the timber rail at the far end of the yards, watching them.

'Thanks, Mrs D!' Milly yelled back.

Poppy rode Crystal over to her. 'Where's Storm?' she asked.

'In there,' Aunt Sophie said, pointing past the wild colts. 'I have the oddest feeling that they know they're related.'

Poppy stood up on her stirrups, balls of her feet pressed hard to the iron as she stared over the railings. Her heart skipped a beat.

Storm was standing quietly in the yard, resting one rear leg, his ears turned forward as he seemed to study the two colts. She wondered if he was silently telling them something, if he'd already managed to calm them.

'He's something special, that brumby of yours,' Aunt Sophie said. 'And if I hadn't seen it today with my own eyes, I don't know I would have believed it.'

Poppy didn't have to ask her aunt what she was talking about because she'd seen it, too. She had no doubt in her mind now that he did know where he was. Barmah was in his blood and it always would be.

She slowly moved Crystal away as the members of the Brumby Association and Uncle Mark climbed up on the rails to check the colts. It was almost time to go home, and that meant having two nights at Starlight Stables and then heading home for the rest of the week.

'Storm's a lucky boy,' Katie mused as they rode along.

Poppy held out a hand and gently touched a low-hanging tree branch.

'Why?' she asked.

'Because he has you, and he always will,' Katie replied.

Poppy craned her neck to see her brumby, just making out his white blaze that stretched down the front of his face to the tip of his nose. She guessed he was lucky. So many of the Barmah brumbies were safe, but for how long? Her Storm was safe forever, and now the two brumbies that they'd helped to rescue would be safe, too.

'Anyone hungry?' Milly asked, interrupting Poppy's thoughts.

Poppy met Katie's eyes and they burst into laughter.

'What?' Milly asked.

'You,' Poppy chuckled. 'It doesn't matter what we're doing, you're always starving!'

Milly suddenly kicked Joe on and flew past them, dodging a tree and spraying them in dirt as she hoofed it away.

'Told you,' Katie groaned as they both wiped their faces and coughed at the dust. 'She always gets us back way better than we could ever get her!'

Poppy looked at Katie's brown, dust-smeared face.

'We'll figure out a way to get her back one day,' she giggled. 'Trust me.'

'You really think so?' Katie sighed.

Poppy leaned over and held out her hand, pinky finger raised. They linked them.

'I don't just think so. I promise.'

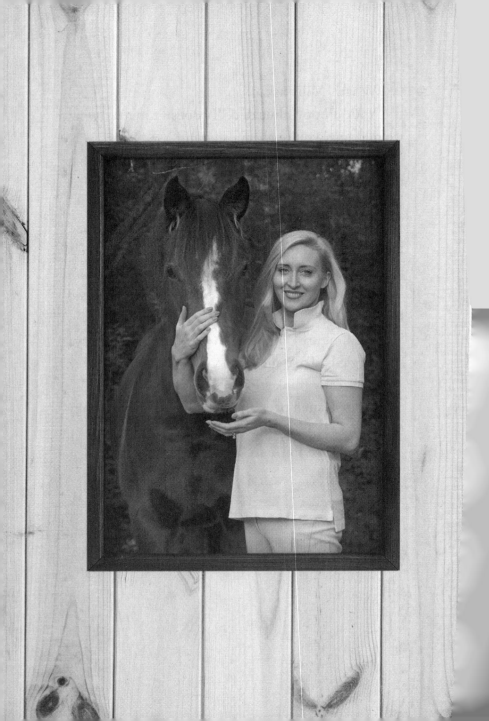

ABOUT THE AUTHOR

As a horse-crazy girl, Soraya dreamed of owning her own pony and riding every day. For years, pony books like *The Saddle Club* had to suffice, until the day she finally convinced her parents to buy her a horse. There were plenty of adventures on horseback throughout her childhood, and lots of stories scribbled in notebooks, which eventually became inspiration for Soraya's very own pony series. Soraya now lives with her husband and children on a small farm in her native New Zealand, surrounded by four-legged friends and still vividly recalling what it felt like to be 12 years old and head over heels in love with horses.

If you are lucky enough to go trail riding or camping on your horse or pony, remember to stay safe! You're best always to ride with a friend, and if you have access to a mobile phone, take it with you. Wearing a fluoro vest will make sure you're seen by other riders or motorists if you're near a road, and if you are away from home or riding a long distance, take a pack with food and water. If you're overnighting somewhere or travelling far, you will need to check ahead to make sure your horse will have access to fresh water. Sometimes it's easy to forget the needs of our four-legged friends at the end of a journey, but they need food and water just as much as we do!

Barmah National Park is home to many small mobs of brumbies. Many reports claim there are 300 heritage horses living in the park; however, locals believe the true number is closer to 100. Currently the Barmah brumbies are safe to stay in their habitat, despite numerous attempts over the past few years to have them removed from the National Park.

If you are ever fortunate enough to visit, it is highly likely you will see a group of brumbies in the wild there. No brumbies were allowed to be mustered from Barmah National Park at the time this book went to print. However, I can imagine a time will come when small numbers are removed to keep the brumby population from increasing. My hope is that this is done by horse lovers, who will have the opportunity to save and re-home those special brumbies that are no longer allowed to live in the wild.

POPPY'S BRUMBY

Poppy's feisty brumby, Storm, hails from the Barmah National Park. He might start out as a handful, but he soon becomes a much-loved horse at Starlight Stables. Brumbies make wonderful domestic horses, with historically calm temperaments and a great work ethic. The Barmah brumbies originate from Clydesdale and Standardbred heritage, which makes them solid-framed horses with strong bones and big, sturdy feet. They are often bay or chestnut coloured, with large white markings on their faces and/or legs.

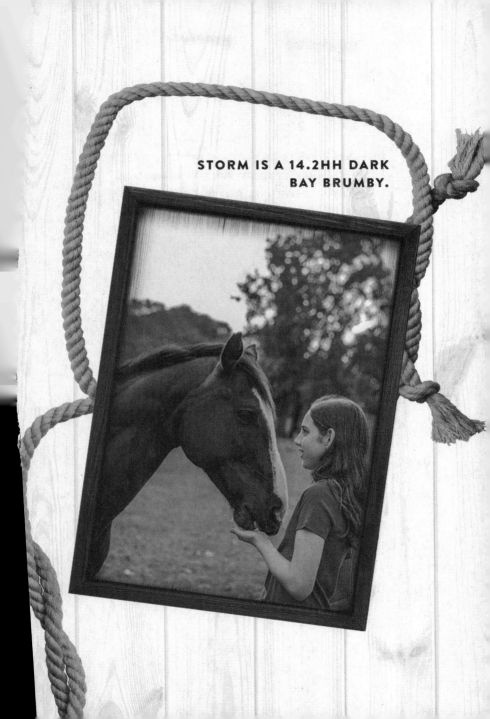

STORM IS A 14.2HH DARK BAY BRUMBY.

PONY DETECTIVES

Poppy is thrilled to be back doing the one
thing she loves – riding horses at Starlight Stables –
especially when her aunt and uncle make all her
dreams come true with a gift of her very own horse.
But there's a catch . . . Poppy must look after the new
scholarship girls. Will the bold and troublesome
Milly and shy, sensible Katie be the pony-mad
friends she's always hoped for? When horses go
missing from the local farms, Poppy worries about
Crystal, her new horse. Will the girls be able to
protect their ponies from the horse thief and find
the missing horses at the same time?

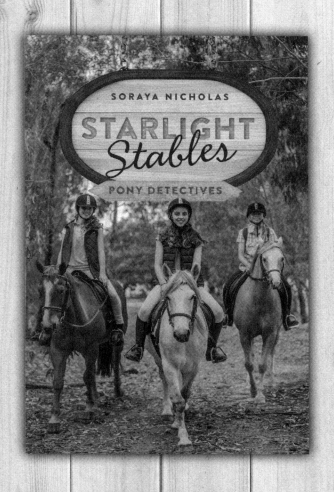

SORAYA NICHOLAS

STARLIGHT
Stables

PONY DETECTIVES

GYMKHANA HIJINKS

Horse-mad friends Poppy, Milly and Katie
are overjoyed to be back at Starlight Stables and
spending every second with their new ponies –
riding, training and having fun while preparing
for their first big Pony Club competition. But when
a rival competitor arrives one day to train with them,
trouble seems to seek the girls out at every turn.
Is it just coincidence? Or is someone trying to
sabotage the three friends' chances of winning?
Can Poppy, Milly and Katie expose their
rival's risky antics in time to save their
chances at the gymkhana?

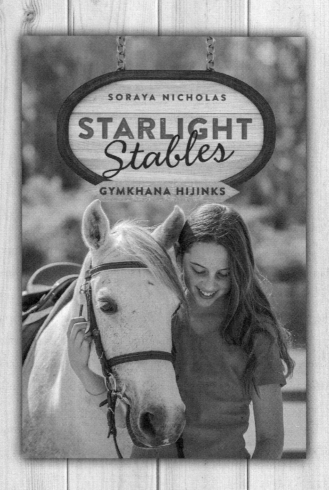

ACKNOWLEDGEMENTS

Penguin Random House would like to give special thanks to Isabella Carter, Emily Mitchell and India James Timms – the faces of Poppy, Milly and Katie on the book covers.

Special thanks must also go to Trish, Caroline, Ben and the team at Valley Park Riding School, Templestowe, Victoria, for their tremendous help in hosting the photoshoot for the covers at Valley Park, and, of course, to the four-legged stars: Alfie and Joe from Valley Park Riding School, and Carinda Park Vegas and his owner Annette Vellios.

Thank you, too, to Caitlin Maloney from Ragamuffin Pet Photography for taking the perfect shots that are the covers.